Those sky-blue eye:

Her full lips parted just a: slept in his arms. Without tho and brushed his mouth again.. ..ei. witn the barest touch.

Susanna gasped but didn't pull away.

He pressed further, making full contact with her lips, flicking his tongue out to taste her.

Sweet. Soft.

A gentle moan came from her throat.

He growled and deepened the kiss, sliding his tongue along the seam of her lush lips until they parted. His tentative licks over the tip her tongue emboldened her, and she soon tangled hers over and under his. She pressed her weight further into his chest, and he wrapped his arms around her.

For the first time in the presence of a woman, he truly relaxed, all thoughts drifting from his head. Desire coursed through his veins, hardening his cock, making him want more than the skittish doe in his arms had likely ever imagined.

Increased pressure where her hands rested on his chest sounded warning bells in his head that she'd lost herself. Much as he wanted to keep her under the spell of desire, he pulled away. He sucked on her bottom lip, groaning as he released it.

He gazed down at the temptress in his hold. Black pupils in those sapphire eyes had blown wide and her lips were plump and red from the kiss. Her cloak had parted enough for him to see her chest heaving.

Susanna swallowed hard and took a step back.

Then another.

He followed, step for step, continuing to hold her.

REVIEW PRAISE FOR
FORGED IN DREAMS AND MAGICK

"A beautifully woven tale about love, choices, courage and destiny, *Forged in Dreams and Magick* is one of the best time-traveling novels. Fans of Gabaldon's *Outlander* will love it." ~ *Bookish Temptations*

~~~

"Delicious Scottish lairds and red-hot steam along with excellent storytelling make for one hellofva read!" ~ *The Indie Bookshelf*

~~~

"A story guaranteed to enthrall with lushly detailed travels into times long gone by. Woven with love, passion, magic and legend, the story had me hooked from the very first chapter." ~ *Read-Love-Blog*

~~~

"I was gripping my iPad like a crazy woman and fanning myself from the smoldering romance. Lawdy!" ~ *The Flirty Reader*

~~~

"Kat Bastion's wonderful debut brings a new voice to the fore. Her voice is strong and unhesitating, very human and real, sometimes young and delicious in her treatment of intimacy and relationship development." ~ *Fangs Wands & Fairydust*

~~~

"An amazing time-traveling tale about love, duty, and honor." ~ *Bitten by Paranormal Romance*

CONTINUED REVIEW PRAISE FOR
FORGED IN DREAMS AND MAGICK

BOOKS BY KAT BASTION

Highland Legends Series

Forged in Dreams and Magick

Bound by Wish and Mistletoe

Born of Mist and Legend
(Releasing in 2014)

Found in Flame and Moonlight
(Releasing in 2015)

Romantic Poetry for Charity

Utterly Loved
(Foreword by Sylvain Reynard)

Bound by
WISH
and
MISTLETOE

A HIGHLAND LEGENDS NOVELLA

KAT BASTION

First paperback edition November 2013

Cover Art © by Stephanie Mooney. All rights reserved.

Publishing History
First Edition, 2013
Print ISBN: 978-0615869254

Published in the United States of America

To every lost soul and dreamer . . .

May you find your happily ever after.

ACKNOWLEDGEMENTS

I've been blessed to have numerous people provide me with insight and guidance during my journey as a writer. To all those who offered support, in gestures big and small, I thank you. A diverse team of people were directly involved in the making of this novel and are mentioned below; however, any errors within the published novel, whether existing there intentionally or not, are my errors alone.

First, deep appreciation goes to my dear friends, daily supporters, and spectacular beta readers, Heather, Misty, and Stone. Every contribution from the belly-aching laughs to the eye-opening critiques is treasured.

Enormous thanks goes to the entire editing team at Finish the Story for their stellar insight, expertise, and suggestions that helped transform *Bound by Wish and Mistletoe* into a sparkling diamond. I'd like to specifically mention Claire Ashgrove. Your dedication continues to amaze me, and I'm honored to be working with you.

Profound gratitude goes to my beloved husband, my most fervent supporter, my best friend, my advisor, my counselor . . . my everything. Thank you for making every day a grand adventure filled with love.

Thank you to all of my friends, fans, supporters, readers, reviewers, and bloggers. Your unending enthusiasm for reading my stories fuels my excitement to write them.

Bound by
WISH
and
MISTLETOE

Chapter One

Scotland—Thirteenth Century

The forest . . . *pulsed.*

Robert Brodie stood in the middle of a bitter winter storm on a mission of debatable absurdity when something rippled through him. The vibration spread across the ground and through the forest canopy like wildfire.

"'Tis a tree like any other. I doona understand Lady Isobel's desire with the wee sapling," Duncan remarked as he approached a Scots fir that was substantial enough to demand his hefty ax.

Robert glanced at his two guardsmen, intrigued that Duncan and Seamus hadn't sensed the odd change in air pressure. The lone twelve-foot pine they'd been tasked to collect from the edge of their holdings had a wide red ribbon woven through its boughs. Snow curled into a funnel beside the tree, whipped high into the air, and disappeared. Cloud cover reflected the last angled light of the sun, casting their frosty world in a silver hue.

Seamus lofted his larger ax into the air and placed a flattened palm on Duncan's chest. "Step aside. 'Tis not the tree, but the want of the lady that matters."

Duncan lowered his head and growled, angling around Seamus. "Touch me again, and I'll cut you down before the tree."

Robert turned away from the two posturing friends and squinted through dense snowfall toward the darkened forest to the southwest. Before a battle, he'd always been able to feel an approaching enemy deep in his belly, and in a similar manner, something raced their way as sure as the cruel wind blowing.

The men quieted, and Robert heard an ax blade whack into soft bark. A second chop thumped, the sound muted by the tremendous mass of the surrounding plant life and the fallen snow.

Inexplicably drawn forward, he trudged through snow that brushed the tops of his worn leather boots. He stopped just before the edge of the small glade. The snowfall continued to thicken. A gust of wind kicked up, and he blinked as fat flakes coated his eyelashes. A twig snapped a few dozen paces ahead in the blinding whiteness.

With silent grace, he unsheathed his sword from the leather scabbard at his hip. His heartbeat slowed in his ears while he forced a measured breath into his lungs.

All of a sudden, hell broke through the trees, clumps of snow launching in every direction from sprung tree branches.

He thrust his sword up, but a split second later, he shot his elbow out—leading with the hilt—to spare an *unarmed* rider on horseback.

The horse reared, and Robert dodged to the side. The rider lost balance and released the reins, falling backward. With his free hand, Robert fisted the rider's cloak at the throat, and in a fluid movement, spun him around, dropped him to the ground, and knelt upon his chest, holding the razor-sharp tip of the sword's blade to his neck.

Wide blue eyes fringed with thick, dark lashes blinked up at him. The intruder swallowed hard and trembled.

Robert scowled, easing back his crushing weight. He moved the point of his sword outward, tugging at the material tied around the rider's neck. The fur-lined cloak fell away, and out spilled long, shining brown hair.

A wee lass was the danger I sensed?

"Explain yourself," he growled.

Her eyes narrowed. "I'll not explain a thing, Highlander.

My concern is not with you. Release me."

"You've breached Brodie lands. Any *concern* you had is now with me."

He assessed her clothing while he pulled the rest of his weight off her. His men had already surrounded them, standing within striking distance of the lass. Their axes raised, they both looked ready to fell her slight frame with a well-placed blade, as if she'd become the tree. Her black cloak was made of the finest woven wool, its lining a rare sable fur. A silk dress, the deep color of sapphire, peeked from beneath the folds. Great wealth had clothed the lass.

Irritated on many levels, Robert grasped her forearm and yanked her up from the ground. Wet snow clung to her entire backside, but she made no move to brush it away. He sheathed his sword, keeping a wary gaze locked onto the lass. Her eyes roved over him in between intermittent glances around the clearing.

Duncan quipped, "I'd hoped to bring home a buck for tomorrow's feast, but I dinna think we'd catch wilder game."

Seamus laughed.

Fast as a heartbeat, a dagger flashed from beneath her cloak. The cold blade pressed against the side of Robert's neck before either of his men caught the movement. Despite her impressive speed, he'd anticipated her action the instant she shifted her body weight. But with the frightened look in her eyes, the hesitation in her execution, and the hard swallow in her throat, he withheld his reaction—he knew she didn't want to hurt him, and he didn't want to injure her unnecessarily.

He slowly raised his hands, giving his men a pointed look and slight head shake as an order to stand down. The returned looks from both men held equal parts amusement and irritation.

"You'll let me be on my way," she said.

"Nay. I will not." He arched a brow and leaned forward, causing her to retract or slice his neck.

She gasped and jerked her hand away. As the steel blade lifted from his neck, Robert grabbed her wrist, spun her around, and clamped his biceps around her bent arms, pinning her dangerous hands to her ribcage.

He growled into her ear, "We could do this all night."

She struggled in his arms, and he tightened his hold until her fight slowed. No matter how hard he squeezed her wrist though, she refused to drop the dagger. Rather than inflict damage for no purpose, he flicked a glance at Seamus then the dagger.

His man moved forward and plucked the weapon from her fingers.

She went wild in Robert's arms again.

He sighed. He'd reluctantly agreed to risk an unforgiving storm to retrieve a damned tree—without explanation by Lady Isobel of what a *Christmas tree* actually was—knowing they couldn't return to their hidden castle until the following day. Dealing with a hellion of a lass had not been in the bargain.

Women everywhere conspire to be the death of me.

He'd foresworn the intimate company of females not even a week ago when three scheming lasses had openly argued for *rights* to him. The young soldiers training in the courtyard had the wisdom to keep their mouths shut. After he snarled a conviction that no woman would *ever* have claim to him, the lasses paled and also went blissfully silent.

He should've known the peaceful respite would be too good to last.

Robert minutely tightened his grip on his struggling captive. When she calmed to a degree, he eased the pressure. "Seamus, fetch that ribbon in the tree."

The lass renewed her efforts to break through his hold. "Nay! Let me go! You doona understand!"

Robert forced her wrists together, and Seamus wound the wide red fabric around them. The lass started to buck and kick within his unyielding arms before Seamus pulled the last knot tight.

Without warning, Robert stepped back. Her own aggressive force threw her backward and dumped her ass-first atop the snow. He chuckled at the intensity of her glare. Although she'd proven amusing when indignant, he thoroughly enjoyed the lass incensed.

She let out an escalating growl as an explosion of movement happened beneath the material of her cloak and gown. They watched a spectacle unfold as she struggled to get up from the snow. With each movement, she buried herself deeper until the only thing showing above the fluffy powder was the dangling end of a bright red ribbon marking its present below, her hands held stiff above the surface as if defiantly refusing to sink in defeat.

He snorted. "Go. Chop down the tree. I'll see to the hellcat."

Seamus chuckled. "Duncan, we must be blessed to earn the better of the two tasks."

"Indeed." Duncan clapped Robert's shoulder. "May you fare well, Commander."

"Does she sound a bit like Lady Isobel?" Seamus asked as they walked away, returning to their task.

"I doona think so," Duncan replied. "But if she possesses half of Lady Isobel's will, he'll have his hands full."

Deep chuckles from his men rose louder then faded off behind him as he considered the strangeness of the day. Fetching a pine tree for another of Lady Isobel's "holiday events" seemed an odd request, but he never questioned his laird's wife. Although she'd been brought here from the future by magick for Iain, their unconventional lady had saved Iain's life. Therefore anything she wanted was already hers. That today's peculiar errand also brought an unexpected woman, added another dimension to an already bewildering mission.

All the while, the infuriated lass fired off a string of incoherent curses from beneath the mound of white. He remained motionless—with the calm patience born of a true military strategist—until her movements ceased and her last sound was uttered.

At the exact moment he knew she'd settled into her circumstance, he took a step closer, allowing the crunch of snow under his boot to alert her. He stared down at the red ribbon. "Do you yield?"

Silence met his question. He knew she hadn't gone unconscious because she still held her hands rigid above the snow. The ribbon began to tremble as she held fast in her obstinance.

"To your left," Seamus called.

A heavy crunch of snow followed. Robert didn't turn, but imagined the pine tree had finally succumbed to its fate. Duncan walked into his peripheral vision, gathering dead limbs from the dry, denser portions of the forest.

Robert waited. He watched his charge . . . as she waited. Neither was happy about the circumstances. Her misfortune in crossing their paths, however, had created a duty of protection for him—both to her and to his clan—which overrode either of their choices in the matter.

A low sound came from the mound of snow, but the message was muffled by the wind whipping around his ears.

"Louder. I dinna hear you."

"Aye. I yield," she growled out.

He smirked, closed a hand around her bound wrists, and dislodged her from the pile of snow. She looked a mess, wet snow clinging to every surface. Her hood had fallen off and snow filled the pouched material. The exposed skin of her chest and face flamed bright red from the cold, and likely, a bit from her anger. Big blue eyes stared up at him until they squinted, long, dark lashes hiding their beauty.

The poor lass had soaked herself through during her headstrong tirade, but he figured it had served a purpose: she'd think twice about threatening him or his men.

"Weel, come on with you." On a final tug, he fully pulled her from the hole in the snow where she stood. Without a sound or ounce of resistance, she let him lead her to a fallen log under denser tree cover, a dozen paces from where their horses, and now her skittish mare, were tied to the lowest branches of an oak.

The spirited lass held her body rigid, her lips in a tight line, as he removed her soaked, heavy cloak and hung it by the hood on a protruding branch near the spot Duncan had prepared for a fire. She shivered in the freezing night air, the damp silk of her dress clinging to the generous curves on her too-slender form. While watching her for signs of regained fight, he untied his rolled plaid from the back of his saddle.

He returned and unfurled the dry material into the air, caught the loose end, and wrapped the wool around her quivering body.

Without a second thought, he pulled her into his arms, tucking her beneath his own cloak to share what warmth he could. Her shoulders went rigid, but after a moment, her tense muscles loosened, and she leaned further into him.

He, too, stiffened his arms and spine in shock, realizing he'd inadvertently given comfort to a lass after his self-preserving vow, but he slowly relaxed at the impossible notion that she'd be like any of the relentless women who'd pursued him. Schemes and motives to escalate social standing were far different than appreciating basic needs for survival.

The lass's shivering stopped, and he pulled back to look down into beautiful eyes that had softened from those of a cornered wolf to those of a lost pup.

With an arm beneath hers and a finger looped through her ribbon binding, he led her to a flattened part of the mossy, fallen trunk and pressed gently on her shoulders until she sat down. Duncan and Seamus approached the far side of the sheltered area with their harvested pine, shaking the snow off its branches as they argued about the best way to truss the limbs up as they'd been instructed.

Two seconds after her teeth-chattering stopped, the lass's mouth opened. "You canna keep me prisoner. You've no idea what evil comes after me. You and your men are not safe."

Robert barked out a laugh as he helped Duncan stack dry wood for the fire. "Ahhh, I see the way of it. You're concerned for *our* safety."

She glanced at Seamus and Duncan. "Aye. Yours and mine."

He arched a brow and gave his companions a pointed look. Had she hit her head? Duncan and Seamus were among the largest in their laird's guard. Robert's own stature bested that of his men in height and breadth by several inches. Never having feared beast or man, he couldn't make sense of her claim.

He turned back to her, assessing her expression. She believed the words she'd spoken. "What's your name, lass?"

She tilted her head, weighing her answer.

He wondered if she'd utter a truth or a lie and carefully watched her eyes. They stayed locked onto his, never straying. She didn't blink. Her body never flinched.

"Susanna."

Truth.

"What's this evil that comes after you, Susanna? Why are you in its sights?" he asked.

Her eyes grew wide, and her gaze drifted to the spot in the trees where she'd come flying into the clearing. Her voice dropped to a whisper as the first sign of fear flashed across her face.

"My father."

Chapter Two

Susanna looked away from the depths of the ominous forest into the eyes of her imposing captor. Frightening memories taunted her mind, and she pinched her eyes shut, willing the thoughts away like she'd always done. She finally inhaled a deep breath, her lungs burning for air.

She focused on the only thing certain to calm her during one of her rioting panic attacks. *Mama.*

"Child it will be all right. We live in a world we cannot control. Live for me. If we live for each other, no one can touch what lies inside."

Her mother placed a hand over the fist Susanna clutched against her chest. With patience, Mama uncurled Susanna's tight fingers and spread them open, covering her chilled hand with her warmer one. "Our hearts hold the greatest treasure. Love. We believe the suffering we endure is temporary, and that God will deliver us from it to a better place. Trust in that."

"But Mama, why does God make us suffer so? Why us . . . at the hands of such hateful men? They enjoy inflicting pain upon us. Why does God allow it?"

Her beautiful mother's blue eyes gazed down at her. "I do not know why. I only know their joy is brief, but ours will be eternal."

Susanna closed her eyes. She gripped her mother's hand and made the only wish she'd ever make, in a prayer bound tight in hope . . . that God would have love embrace them.

Something touched Susanna, pulling her out of her poignant reverie. She fluttered her lashes open to find her captor had hooked his finger under her chin and lifted her face. His lips hovered above hers. Coal-black hair fell like a silken drape, brushing against the high points of harsh cheek bones. His dark brown eyes stared deep into her soul.

Her breath caught. No one had looked at her with that kind of depth besides her mother. Shocked by the oddity, she stared up at him. Compassion and understanding washed across his face. Had she not seen those same things in her mother, she wouldn't have recognized them.

"Your father will never harm you again," he said, his voice almost a growl.

Susanna laughed. The man knew nothing, yet spoke with confidence, as if he commanded the world. She narrowed her eyes, remembering what he was . . . what they all were. "Aye. He'll not hurt me. No man ever will." She jerked her chin away from his touch, keeping a wary gaze leveled on him.

The Highlander pulled his hand back and straightened to his full height. He stared at her with scorching intensity.

His red-haired companion approached. "We've secured the pine."

"Good," her captor replied, not looking away from her. "We'll camp here for the night."

A shiver traveled through her. She did her best not to show the weakness, but his eyes traveled down her body in response to the involuntary action.

"Finish buildin' the fire, Duncan. Susanna needs the warmth of it."

Susanna glanced beyond their shelter into the growing darkness as snowflakes fell more closely together. The storm continued to help camouflage her tracks, but if those who pursued her discovered the direction of her escape . . .

"You canna light a fire!" she shouted.

Duncan looked up from his squatting position and stood, still holding a large piece of wood in his hand. The other man, the one called Seamus, had been unfastening something from the back of a horse but stopped and turned fully toward her. Both men walked closer until they stood just behind her captor.

No one spoke. They merely stared at her as if she'd grown another head atop her shoulders. As the seconds ticked by with not one of them looking away—or blinking—she began to wonder if she had.

Duncan broke the silence. "She supposes to tell the commander how to best handle a situation. Bold."

"Aye," Seamus replied, a smirk twitching the corners of his mouth. "She speaks against the great leader of our guard, somethin' no *man* has ever dared, let alone a woman."

Their commander dropped his head, staring at a spot on the ground between her boots and his. He took a deep breath as his jaw muscles clenched. "Do you seek to join her in such folly?"

Both of his men burst into laughter. Duncan clapped his leader on the shoulder as they turned to leave. "Nay, Commander. We merely paused to commit a rare moment to memory."

She'd had enough of people talking about her as if she wasn't there. Cloistered her entire existence, she hadn't dared to speak against a man to his face. But she'd abandoned that life.

A strength rose from deep within her as she vowed to be the liberated woman she had set free in her new world. "I'll speak to you in any manner I choose. Do you have a name? I tire of callin' you Highlander, and I refuse to call you Commander."

He roared with laughter. The rare sound caught her off guard, and her lips twitched. She pressed them into a firm line, furrowing her brow, remembering they were the enemy—all of them.

"Only my men call me Commander." His lips twisted into a smirk. "You may address me as Commander if you ever choose to show such respect. My friends call me Robert. You held a blade to my throat"—he lifted his fingers and gently touched the spot where a red mark remained—"but I'll allow any address you choose . . . for now."

"Can friends be untied?" she asked, hopeful.

He chuckled. "You misunderstand, lass. I doona keep female friends. Call me Robert if it suits you, but you're simply a stray lass, and I'm your obligated escort . . . nothin' else."

To her left, his men had a sizable fire started. Much as she longed for its warmth, a daunting anxiety grew within her like the orange flames that licked up from beneath the logs. "They'll find us," she said softly, staring into the growing blaze.

Robert drew closer and squatted in front of her. She tore her gaze from the fire and looked into his dark eyes. Light and shadows danced across his features—a strong jaw line, straight nose, dark stubble below chiseled cheek bones—making his face look even more fierce.

"You're safe from harm now, Susanna. If your father or his men chase you, they'd be fools to do so in this storm. We canna return to the castle 'til the morrow, but you'll do so under our protection."

She lifted her bound hands in front of his face. "As a prisoner?"

Robert laughed. "If I unbind your hands, will you promise not to injure my men or flee?"

He asked a lot. She could guarantee neither. The only promise she'd ever made had been to her mother, and she intended to keep her word at all costs. One thing she'd grown adept at, however, was lying.

"You hesitate too long. *Friend.*" He winked and tapped a finger to the tip of her nose. "Maybe we'll release you once you get those wild ideas out of your head."

She snapped her teeth at his extended finger, but he yanked it out of her reach.

"Be careful, Susanna. I'll easily bind that luscious mouth of yours as well."

Her jaw dropped open. She snapped it shut. With her recent luck, one vicious retort would tempt him to make good on his threat the instant she let her thoughts fly free.

He waited, watching her, but she returned her gaze to the fire, acting uninterested in any further communication with him.

She sighed. If only she'd angled her mare a degree to the east or the west, she wouldn't have come across a soul. A straight ride for a day or two, unseen by anyone, and she would've never been under the power of another man again.

By stumbling across Robert and his men, she'd inadvertently dashed her hopes of guaranteed freedom. What she'd been left with were chances. Earlier today she'd seized upon a chance to escape certain doom from her father. She'd simply have to keep steadfast watch for another opportunity.

"Are you hungry?" Robert asked.

Susanna followed the sound of his voice to where he stood by her horse that had been tethered with the others. He'd opened her satchel and now held up the parcel of food she had carefully wrapped for her journey. Since the package had lain at the bottom of her belongings, he'd obviously satisfied himself that she had no further weapons.

She shook her head. Robert shrugged, but surprisingly took her rations with him as he walked beyond his men. Duncan and Seamus sat on separate blankets spaced a few feet apart from both each other and the fire. Robert lowered down onto another plaid, which confused her because he'd given her the one she huddled under. She glanced at the horses to confirm hers was missing; he sat upon her father's red-and-black clan plaid.

He knows. Robert had to have figured out who her father was by her MacEalan plaid; Broc had boasted about wearing the newly adopted attire at diplomatic events over the last year.

She had no idea what outsiders thought of the tyrant who subjugated the women in his family, but she knew what those in her clan thought. They worshiped him. His ruthless hand had kept them safe from English domination, and to the people under his care, he'd become nothing short of a god.

Robert watched her with unconcealed interest. She narrowed her eyes, irritation brewing at the blatant rudeness of his confiscating her possessions. First her dagger. Now her rations. The only consolation was that he hadn't taken a bite of her food, but instead had spread the small bread round, wedge of cheese, and her now quartered red apple upon the linen wrapping. He lifted his hand, offering her a piece of apple.

She shook her head again, refusing to be lured closer to the stranger with her food. The curious, soft expression on his face calmed her to a degree, but his very *maleness* overrode the alarming instinct to trust him.

As she stared at Robert, he held her gaze but addressed his men. "Duncan, Seamus, you must be hungry from your hard work."

His men exchanged glances.

"Aye," Duncan said with a guarded tone.

"Aye," Seamus added, the corners of his mouth twitching once again into a smirk.

Robert passed part of her food to his men, never breaking his assessing eye contact with her. Without asking, he gave away provisions she'd taken great care to steal and hide for her journey. Goading her. Yet with the intense gaze he blazed her way, and not one morsel of food nearing his mouth, he behaved only in small part like the men she'd been exposed to. Something more, an undercurrent of indecipherable emotion beneath his inconsiderate façade, threw her off-balance.

She gritted her teeth and forced herself to stare into a fire that had calmed without stoking. None of its heat managed to reach where she still sat upon the log, and an uncontrollable shiver racked through her from head to toe.

Aggravated by the grief the men seemed intent to cause, but reminding herself it was endurable compared to what she'd been through, she relented and stalked over to her plaid. She quelled her ire by realizing if they'd intended to camp for the night, they had food, and she'd take from them in kind before hunger became an issue. Without giving Robert the satisfaction of a glance or a word, she took a corner that he'd left clear, closest to the fire. She sighed and opened the front of her wrap, pulling in the fire's remaining heat.

Robert snorted. "Susanna, doona suffer on my account. Eat. We've still a journey ahead of us on the morrow, and you'll need your strength."

From the corner of her eye, she saw movement. Robert moved the last of her bread and cheese near her, his fingers balancing a wedge of apple on the very top. By the time she looked up from the tiny pile of food, he'd reclined back, the opening of a waterskin between his lips as he drank.

Her throat was dry. Susanna swallowed, needing some of what he held to quench her thirst, but she refused to open her mouth. She'd never asked a man for anything . . . and had no intention of beginning.

Robert's eyes lit with mischief. "Would you like some water, Susanna?"

She nodded before her verbal response fully formed. He leaned forward and held the neck of the waterskin up. Her lips pursed around the opening, and cold, pure water filled her mouth. Each crisp, quenching swallow tasted more amazing than the one before. Once she'd had her fill, she tipped her chin up to stop the flow.

"There. Not so difficult," he said.

She eyed him in silence for long moments, unable to read his behavior as kindness or mockery. Her gaze slowly dropped to the food. The beast had left her a fraction of what she'd packed, but the small portion would suffice for the night. She tried to grasp the apple wedge with two fingers, reasoning it was foolish to let any of it go to waste for her pride, but with her wrists bound so tightly, maneuvering to pick it up proved awkward.

"Allow me," he said.

Robert put the apple aside, and she watched as he tore the hard bread into smaller pieces before lifting the first bite up to her. Her mouth fell open over the shock of a man tending to a woman with such care, which gave him the perfect opportunity to place the food between her lips.

It surprised her when he took great effort not to touch her. In fact, he leaned so close into her body, his nearness afforded her some of his heat without any trace of contact.

She closed her mouth and chewed slowly, staring at him.

"You doona need to worry, Susanna. You're under our protection. When we're back at the castle, all your fears will fade away."

Robert stared at her with an intensity that made her breath catch.

Nervous, she glanced toward Duncan and Seamus, but they'd already settled onto their plaids, each man facing outward, their backs to the fire. Both happened to be directly between her and her horse. Even if she managed to slip by Robert, she doubted his men would sleep through any escape attempt.

Since she had no choice, she tried to accept her present circumstances. That his men appeared to have no interest in her personally encouraged her. Robert showing her attention, but doing so with a respect she'd only seen from her clansmen toward her father . . . puzzled her.

With a crackling thud, the fire-decayed logs fell, settling into the red glow below. One of the logs reignited in dancing orange flames. Weary from the eventful day, she gazed up into the dark forest canopy. Lush, green pine branches guarded their small party for the night, shielding them from a wind that swirled tiny snowflakes into the darkness beyond.

"Susanna."

She glanced back at Robert as he lowered down a bite of cheese that he'd apparently held out to her while she'd been daydreaming.

"You've nothin' to fear from us. We're not brutes like Broc MacEalan. No harm will come to you."

So he does *know of my father.*

The harshness of Robert's dark features softened. His eyes held tenderness, like Mama's. She shook her head, refusing to believe Robert's words and actions. Men were born as selfish, hateful creatures. Mama had said so. Warnings had been drilled into Susanna for her own protection, and she'd clung to those rules and beliefs, because she'd needed them to survive with each breath pulled into her lungs.

"Aye, Susanna," he continued. "I doona know what demons you've had to fight, but the nightmare ends tonight. No man will ever harm you again."

As a rising fear took hold, she blinked and gazed deep into his eyes. He professed things that made her nervous. The calm, low tone of his voice and his serious expression frightened her in a new way, causing an unsettling flutter in her chest.

She closed her eyes and shook her head harder, shutting out the unbidden anxiety floating from her belly into her throat.

His warm hand gently curved over both of hers, and she opened her watery eyes. Angry at her uncontainable reactions, she blinked away the hot tears.

Robert lifted his other hand and caught a falling tear with a feather's touch. "I'll protect you, Susanna," he vowed.

At his words and the unexpected caress, all of her thoughts clarified into a single point. She swallowed hard as a suspicion of his intentions hit her. Her voice fell to a whisper. "And who will protect me from you?"

Chapter Three

Robert let the startling question hang between them—for he had no answer to give. He stared in awe at a creature more like an angry bird with a broken wing than a prowling cat in a ball gown. She bore a determination found in the best of his men, yet she harbored a past that she'd fled from at all costs.

Never in his life had he felt compelled to protect a woman beyond his role as commander. A heart that had only ever thundered for his clan suddenly stuttered, and he needed to ease the burning ache developing in his chest.

With quiet patience, he again lifted the cheese that he held between his fingers, and Susanna opened her mouth obediently. Her many darted glances toward her horse told him she would flee at the first opportunity. The fear she held was so great, she remained a danger to him, to his men, and to herself.

After Susanna chewed and swallowed the last bite of food, she quenched her thirst again with water, cradling the bottom of the pouch with her fingers while he held it to her lips.

Her gaze drifted away from him as he brushed the crumbs from her plaid, and she straightened her spine, leaning toward the dying fire. The unforgiving cold night crept in, burrowing past his cloak and through his linen shirt. Although she had his plaid wrapped around her, the dress she wore beneath had to still be damp from her fruitless battle in the snowbank. He sighed and drew her down, curling her body against his, facing away from the horses and his men. She struggled from the moment of contact, bucking against his hold.

"Shhh . . . I only intend to prevent your freezin' to death in the night." He wrapped an arm over both of hers, caging her, ensuring if she made a single move while he slept, he'd stop her before she made the second.

An exasperated sigh escaped her lips, but the muscles in her body eased, and she relaxed back into his chest. As she stilled against him, he tucked a folded arm beneath his head. The pull of exhaustion tugged at him, and he gave in to the luring fall of sleep, knowing the men at his back would alternate guard through the night. At his front, the woman in his arms had calmed, secured for the moment. The deep ravine beyond her provided all of them a natural barrier to danger in the darkness.

First light filtered a glow through Robert's eyelids. He awoke to Susanna snuggled into his side, facing him while she remained sound asleep. Her full pink lips were slightly parted, her chest rising and falling in gentle rhythm. Her fierce edge had been tamed in the comfort of his arms—even if it was because she was unconscious.

He'd never seen a more attractive woman. *Angered or pacified.*

The women who'd relentlessly pursued him had always pressed into his arms, argued among their peers over who had the rights to a dance, or schemed throughout their day to bump into him. *Literally.* He'd always seen through their ruse and had grown tired of women—had quite vocally sworn off women—in an attempt to stem the tide. His clansmen had laughed, giving sometimes sarcastic, but mostly empathetic, condolences. The women only persevered, seeing an even greater challenge.

Yet, in a rare moment of serenity during a fierce winter storm in the middle of the forest, one woman who'd nearly run him down now lay peacefully in his arms. Every word she'd spoken, and each action she'd taken, indicated that within his embrace was no place she wanted to be. In the sticky web of sleep, however, her instincts had sought him out, telling him otherwise.

Susanna had no idea, but she'd already become his.

In a twist of fate, a woman who wanted nothing to do with him had suddenly become the only woman in the world who would ever do.

A clear, blue sky opened through the treetops overhead, and birds sang in the new day with joy. He heard his men rustle behind him. A freshened fire crackled, signaling they'd been up a while.

Susanna stirred quietly in his arms. Her eyelids fluttered open.

He gazed down into her widening eyes and slowly grinned.

To his shock, she screamed, nearly piercing his eardrums, and shoved away. Her sudden momentum rolled her several times until she scrambled to her feet, the hem of her dress catching beneath her boots.

The direction of her unexpected flight slammed his heart into his throat as he helplessly watched her stumble toward the ravine. He lunged forward trying to grab her, but she stepped back from him in fear. Loose rocks clattered down into the ravine, punctuating the grave danger.

"Susanna! Stop!"

His panicked shout did enough to broadcast the impending danger to her, and she froze. Her eyes went wide with panic, and her entire body shook on the unstable edge. She turned her head slightly to the side and darted a glance down, her chest heaving.

"Susanna. Doona turn your head. Look at me."

She slowly turned her head toward him, exactly as he'd instructed.

It took a staggering amount of willpower to remain where he stood, projecting a feeling of calmness that he in no way had. "Good, lass. On your right leg, move all your weight forward. Aye. Lean a little more . . ."

He stepped forward when her gaze grew unfocused while she concentrated. If that edge gave way, he would die before he let her go down with it.

With his gaze locked onto those bright blue eyes, he lifted his hands, and she instantly glanced down and grasped them. The moment they touched, he yanked her into his arms at the same time she jumped into them. As she clung to him, more decomposing granite fell loose behind her, clattering against the rock face as the shards bounced into the chasm below.

He rubbed his hands up and down her arms as she trembled. "Shhh . . . 'tis all right, lass. You're safe now."

Suddenly, she gave a hard pound to his chest with her bound fists and jerked backward. "You dinna tell me such a deadly threat was right next to us." She wrenched out of his embrace and stomped back toward their camp.

"I dinna think you'd run in the *opposite direction of our horses!*"

Susanna spun around and squared off with him, her entire body rigid. The scowl on her face deepened, her brows drawing lower over her eyes. "Doona think about what I will and will not do. I alone decide my actions."

Robert laughed and shook his head. She growled and resumed her course—away from him.

He refused to tear his gaze from the intriguing woman; he didn't want to miss a thing.

Duncan and Seamus watched the exchange with silent interest. She strode between the two men seated on the ground, as if the formidable warriors didn't exist.

Robert strolled back as Susanna marched straight for the horses. She went right past her mare, and with clumsy determination despite her bound hands, rifled through the satchel on the next horse, which happened to belong to Seamus.

The animal nickered, swinging his head around. Robert stopped his advance and crossed his arms, a slight smile twitching at the corners of his mouth while he witnessed an inevitable scene unfold.

Seamus shot up from the ground and stalked toward her. "Och! Unhand my horse!"

Susanna ignored the warning as if she'd gone deaf in both ears.

Seamus laid a hand on hers to stop her.

Robert flinched. He used every tightened muscle in his body to remain where he stood as another man touched her. The sudden possessiveness surprised him.

She turned on Seamus, teeth bared. "*Unhand. Me.* You arrogant men helped yourselves to my food last night. I'm repayin' the favor."

From the ground where he still reclined, Duncan roared in laughter. Robert's smile grew wider as Seamus's jaw dropped. Despite the fact that the angered warrior towered over the petite lass, Seamus pulled back and remained a few inches from her, his fists opening and closing in clear frustration while she ransacked his belongings.

Finding no food, Susanna moved on to the next horse, Duncan's. Duncan remained on his plaid, an arm over a bent knee, an amused expression on his face. Seamus calmed, his belongings no longer being violated. Robert snorted. The first woman he'd ever had the pleasure to irritate entertained him with each successive move she made.

He crossed his arms and leaned against a tree as she continued on to his horse. He knew what she would find there. After rummaging through his scant belongings, she pulled out an unremarkable, short length of shaved pine and dropped it back in.

"None of you have food?" she whined, turning back toward them.

Duncan replied, "Aye, lass. 'Tis over here. We broke fast while you slept like a newborn bairn."

She glared at Duncan and stormed toward him. He shifted, looking even more relaxed, his arms held together loosely over his bent knees. Large pieces of dried meat and bread lay on the corner of the plaid.

"Whose portion is that?" she asked, nodding toward the food.

Robert answered her. "Yours." He didn't add that it was his portion as well. She needed her strength, and he could wait.

She narrowed her eyes, her nostrils flaring. "Aye, by all rights, 'tis mine."

Robert laughed as she confiscated both of their shares. She whisked her meal over to a sheltered area—as far away from them as possible while still in line of sight—and devoured it.

He and the men broke camp while Susanna wandered out of view behind a thicket. He gave her all the privacy she needed, figuring it was the least he could do in light of everything he couldn't grant her.

Fifteen minutes later, she returned, stomping into the clearing. Upon seeing her deep scowl as she shook her bound hands high in the air, he had to tap into his discipline as a warrior not to break into a smile or outright laughter. She looked glorious.

He smirked. Apparently, he was unable to contain it all.

She glared at him with the heat of a thousand fires. "You've no idea how difficult it is to . . . to do *things* tied up like this."

"I have some idea."

"Where are your men?" She looked around. "Where's *my horse*?" she yelled, advancing on him.

"Ahead of us," he replied, holding back a smile. The more frustrated and angry she became, the more he found that he liked her. And he suspected she would find great displeasure in that fact.

He pulled her cloak from the branch where he'd hung it last night. The material had completely dried and still held warmth from the morning's fire. He spread his arms wide, holding it open for her.

She cocked her head, waited, and sighed before stepping up to him and turning around. He wrapped the cloak around her shoulders and fastened the ties at her neck. While close to her, a light floral fragrance drifted up that he hadn't detected before, and he inhaled deeply, drawn to her scent.

With care not to startle her, he gently placed his hands

on her shoulders and dropped his head down, resting his lips on the chilled shell of her ear. Her muscles tensed beneath his hands.

"You needn't be afraid of me, Susanna," he murmured. "I give you my word, every action I make around you will be for your protection . . . or pleasure."

The lass shuddered within his arms, and her head tilted to the side, dropping slightly. She turned and looked up at him, her dark-brown, tousled hair framing a face almost painfully beautiful.

An intensifying blush deepened the pink on her cheeks. "I've never known either. You ask me to trust you. When you doona trust me, how can I?" She lowered her gaze to her hands.

Robert looked down between them at the red ribbon binding her wrists. She spoke the truth. After all he'd observed about her since their first explosive encounter, he doubted she would harm him or his men, as long as she didn't feel threatened by them.

"You're right, lass."

He pulled a dagger from the inside of his boot. With precision, he sliced through the fragile fabric, and the long length unfurled, fluttering to the ground on the breeze.

The jerk of the blade pulled her forward, and she fell into him, bracing her weight against his chest. She glanced up, wide-eyed at the sudden contact.

Those sky-blue eyes mesmerized him. Her full lips parted just as they'd done while she'd slept in his arms. Without thought, he dipped his head and brushed his mouth against hers with the barest touch.

Susanna gasped but didn't pull away.

He pressed further, making full contact with her lips, flicking his tongue out to taste her.

Sweet. Soft.

A gentle moan came from her throat.

He growled and deepened the kiss, sliding his tongue along the seam of her lush lips until they parted. His tentative licks over the tip her tongue emboldened her, and she soon tangled hers over and under his. She pressed her weight further into his chest, and he wrapped his arms around her.

For the first time in the presence of a woman, he truly relaxed, all thoughts drifting from his head. Desire coursed through his veins, hardening his cock, making him want more than the skittish doe in his arms had likely ever imagined.

Increased pressure where her hands rested on his chest sounded warning bells in his head that she'd lost herself. Much as he wanted to keep her under the spell of desire, he pulled away. He sucked on her bottom lip, groaning as he released it.

He gazed down at the temptress in his hold. Black pupils in those sapphire eyes had blown wide and her lips were plump and red from the kiss. Her cloak had parted enough for him to see her chest heaving.

Susanna swallowed hard and took a step back.

Then another.

He followed, step for step, continuing to hold her. He feared if he let go, she'd fall over, the way she heavily swayed.

She blinked up at him in shock, like he'd stolen her most precious treasure . . . and she couldn't believe she'd let him. Her mouth opened. She shut it wordlessly, lifting her fingertips and brushing them over the lips he'd just ravished.

"Aye, Susanna. That was only a hint of the pleasure I spoke of."

She took a deep breath and let out a long shaky sigh.

He did the same, rattled to his core by a woman—something he'd never imagined possible.

Chapter Four

Susanna stared up at Robert, unable to grasp the fragmented thoughts whirling around in her head as her heart thundered in her ears, her chest, and—to her extreme shock—between her legs. How could her body feel this way?

How could a *man* be the cause of it?

Robert stood easily as tall and broad as any warrior in her clan, if not more so. His dark, silken hair cascaded over his shoulders, a braid hanging from each temple. Eyes so dark they appeared smoke black had gazed down at her when he embraced her with gentle care. Harsh angles in his cheek bones and jaw that had once seemed sinister had changed into something . . . *not at all offensive.*

Her gaze fell to his mouth—an amazing mouth that had seconds ago done wondrous things to her with the merest of touches. She pulled her fingers away from her still-tingling lips and looked down at his chest, shaking her head. The fresh perspective on what a man could be—what no man she'd encountered had ever been—confused her.

Men were selfish bastards who took what they wanted, leaving destruction and despair in their wake. She took a deep, clearing breath, vowing to remember the true nature of men.

A puzzling flash of compassion lit Robert's eyes as he pulled away, rubbing her upper arms. "Come, lass. We've to catch up with the men."

As soon as he broke contact, she instantly missed his strength and warmth. Dismayed by her out-of-control feelings, she pulled her cloak tighter around her and looked beyond him to register again that only Robert's horse remained.

"You let them take my mare." She spun around, remembering he'd said so. But the reality of how they'd now travel escaped her, since Robert had thoroughly muddled her thoughts with the first kiss to ever grace her lips.

"She's with my men," he replied, his tone patient as he mounted his horse.

While she still worked to process what had happened between them, Robert extended a hand down to her. She stared at it. A surprising new part of her wanted to accept his offer, yet she hesitated with everything she'd been trained to believe. Ignoring the ingrained alarm bells in her mind, she closed her eyes and slid her arm into his grip, leaping into unknown territory.

Robert closed a strong hand around her forearm and hoisted her up, seating her in front of him on the enormous stallion. She shifted in the cage of his arms, trying to distance herself from intimate contact without toppling to the ground. Although Robert had freed her hands, her legs had become tangled in her dress, curled to one side.

Despite her struggles, he tucked her tight against him, rendering her immobile. Exhausted from the effort, not to mention her lack of sound sleep over the last several nights, she slumped back into his chest.

His weight shifted forward, and his hot breath tracked across her ear, sending chills down her entire right side. "Aye, just relax, lass. Save your fight for later."

The tone in his voice rippled a cascade of heated goose bumps over her skin and spread warmth inward, deep inside her body. She swallowed hard, concerned about his meaning. "I thought you meant to protect me. Whatever would I need to fight for?" she asked, needing to allay her fear of the unknown.

A low chuckle rumbled out as he sat more upright, sparing her from the heart-pounding threat of overheating.

"You'll see soon enough that sometimes fightin' happens with protectin'. Were it not so, somethin' would be verra wrong in the world."

She shook her head, thoroughly confused.

Robert tightened his hold on the reins, and the horse opened into a gallop, quickly covering the distance over the snow-covered ground of a great meadow. Susanna closed her eyes against the cold wind in her face, inhaling the fresh mineral scent in the air. She licked her lips, almost tasting her freedom, relieved they finally headed away from the threat which most assuredly chased her.

His stallion brought them into another section of sparsely treed land, and within minutes, they encountered Duncan and Seamus on their horses. They led her mare and the horse that towed their pine tree in a pole-and-canvas litter they'd harnessed behind the animal. His men guided them wide around more densely treed areas, keeping their cargo free from snagging on the surrounding brush.

Her gaze remained fixed upon the bound tree, and her brow furrowed as she wondered why they'd do such a thing. Unused to voicing spontaneous questions, she held her tongue about the oddity.

However, the stark silence amid a company of men unsettled her. *Being* in the company of men—and in such close contact with one particular man—made her increasingly nervous.

Images of how it felt to be held by Robert, to be affected so intimately everywhere when only his lips had touched her ear, and her mouth, replayed in her mind. She swallowed hard and took a deep breath as she scanned the forest, looking for something to distract her mind, but not finding it in the monotonous scenery.

Somewhere within her, a brave thread snapped taut, and she forewent her curiosity about the tree, delving straight into her strongest interest. "Tell me of your clan, Robert."

His body shifted, but he didn't reply. She looked up, and he glanced down at her before looking ahead again. "I doona understand the question. 'Tis a family like any other. Children laugh and play, women tempt men with their charms, and our warriors protect them all, keepin' them safe from harm."

"Oh," she said. It sounded like a dream. The picture he painted was nothing like the brutal, frightening world of tyranny she'd fled. She gripped her arms around her midsection, painfully aware that she'd been born into the wrong clan. But then, she wouldn't have been with Mama . . . or been born into a Scottish clan at all. Unfortunately, her very existence was due to the one man who'd tormented them both.

Robert transferred the reins to one hand and wrapped his free arm around her waist, pulling her tighter into his protective warmth. His voice softened to just above a whisper. "Susanna, what did your father do to you?"

She stiffened, her spine going rigid.

Robert's chin dropped, touching the top of her head. "If it distresses you, doona speak of it."

His gentle tone calmed her. Too many unexplainable things coursed through her mind. All the men in her clan, and all those visitors she'd met, followed the same proper decorum and wielded the same charms as her father did—*in public.* Her mother had warned her that all men harbored the same beast inside.

They all wear pretty masks that come off in private, Susanna.

With only her mother's advice to guide her, she kept silent. For all she knew, the dominant stranger who held her had eaten at her father's table. He might even share her father's beliefs. Men were the enemy. And even though Robert showed her unwarranted kindness, once he discovered half-English blood ran through her veins, his compassionate feelings toward her would surely harden.

"I doona wish to," she stated.

Robert tightened both of his upper arms around her shoulders for a few brief seconds then relaxed them. The surprising action comforted her heart, like a hug from Mama. But her roiling mind rapidly transformed his embrace into just another cage. She knew all too well that one didn't need bound wrists to feel imprisoned.

She forced her mind to calm, silencing questions she'd rather not think of, let alone answer. A long hour stretched into two before they reached the edge of the vast section of forest.

Another broad, open field spanned ahead of them. The dark ribbon of a year-round stream flowed to their left, despite encroaching snow and ice. Duncan and Seamus dismounted and led the four horses under their care to the rippling water.

Robert swung to the ground and reached his arms up, slightly lifting his eyebrows. Unaware of a safer means to dismount with her legs tangled in her dress, she leaned toward him, placing her hands on his shoulders, and their gazes locked as he lowered her down.

Her breath caught under the unexpected power of his gaze. It seemed each time he looked into her eyes, he saw deeper inside of her. She forced herself to look away, needing to find the means to breathe normally again.

The jagged snowcapped mountains off in the distant northwest had remained the same as they'd journeyed north and east—the same direction she'd been headed. She glanced back to the south and saw dark storm clouds gathering on the horizon.

"Why did we stop?" she asked. No shelter appeared within sight, and she grew restless with pent-up anxiety. The clear weather they'd had throughout the day afforded her pursuers the same effortless travel Robert and his small company benefited from.

"We stop because we wait. While we wait, we hunt," he said.

Robert tied his horse to an old oak snag alongside the rest of the horses. Seamus and Duncan each unfastened a bow and quiver from their saddle packs.

"Wait for what?" she asked, stepping closer to them.

A biting wind gust whipped her cloak open. She grasped the edges, hugging the material around her. Robert moved to shield her, buffeting her from the cold. He lifted a hand to her cheek, feathering fingertips across her skin in a caress.

The storm clouds that pressed into her view of the sky

fell short of the intensity in Robert's dark eyes as he gazed down at her. Strands of his black hair whipped across his face an instant before the swirling wind blew them back again.

"You'll see with your own eyes. All things reveal themselves in time, lass," he said.

Stunned by the kindness in his voice, she blinked up at a man who reminded her of Mama. Wise. Caring.

She narrowed her eyes, unable to believe a man could have the same qualities as Mama, a woman who'd become a saint in her eyes, the one person who'd been subjected to unimaginable torment and had endured it all for her. Mama had wished to spare Susanna the same fate and, in protection, warned her about men. *All men.*

Robert turned back to his men. Duncan stood in a relaxed stance, facing his commander. Seamus pulled each arrow from his quiver, examining the steel points on the tips.

"We'll stay here with the horses," Robert said. "You circle around to the other end of the stand of trees. If you flush any beasts this way, we'll be ready."

Duncan squinted at Susanna. "We? This woman had a blade to your throat yesterday. Now you hunt together?"

Expressionless, Robert glanced at Susanna. "Do you plan to attack me, lass?"

She opened her hands and held out cold-pinked palms. "With what weapon?"

All three men stared at her for a long moment. Seamus broke the silence with sudden laughter. "Come, Duncan. We'll kill a prize stag long before it has a chance to run this way. Robert's sure to have his hands full."

Robert gave a heavy sigh. He glared at the two men as they jogged left into thicker foliage and disappeared.

"What did they mean when they said that you'll have your hands full?" she asked.

He leveled a deadpan look at her. She waited for him to respond. After a moment, his expression softened, and he let out another sigh, shaking his head. "Doona concern yourself with the teasin' of men, Susanna."

She scowled. She didn't care what men thought, but she

had become their captive by *their* authority. No stranger to imprisonment, she learned everything possible from men who forced her to abide by their will—knowledge enabled escape.

Robert came up behind her, blocking the unrelenting wind, and placed his hands on her shoulders. He led her to a gargantuan pine with twin trunks that sprouted from the ground, and he turned, pulling her shoulders to his chest as he leaned back against one of the trunks.

The shock of being as close to Robert as they'd been on horseback—without necessity—sent her heart racing. She tried to pull away, but his hands gripped her upper arms, holding her tight.

His silken hair brushed against her cheek as his lips pressed down on the top of her head. "You needn't fight me, Susanna. Nothin' will happen between us."

His statement surprised her. "Nothin' will happen?"

He dropped his head, soft lips barely touching the top of her ear. Hot breath fanned down across her ear and neck, and its heat flowed straight into her veins, settling down between her legs. She shifted at the sudden discomfort, but the sensation only intensified with her movement.

"I've never taken from a woman what she didn't offer. I'll not start now." He dipped his head further and placed a kiss beneath her ear that set her skin on fire. "Anythin' you want me to have, you'll offer. If I have my way, you will *beg* me to take it."

She couldn't catch her breath. A throbbing pulse pounded between her thighs, and some wild part of her *wanted* to offer, *wanted* to beg. She had no idea what to beg for, but everything about the man holding her close— touching her more intimately than she'd ever imagined a man doing—made her *want*.

An ingrained resolve shattered the bone-melting sensual haze. Her survival depended on her keeping a clear head. "I'll do neither," she scoffed.

His rich laughter boomed out, wrapping itself around her like a warm embrace. "Aye, lass. I think you'll do both. Soon . . . and often. I'm verra fond of the fight in you though."

Robert loosened his hold, as if making good on his promise. She relaxed on a slow sigh, but the panicked pressure in her head eased faster than the disconcerting throb in the most intimate of places.

The quiet minutes unnerved her as she stood within his embrace, his hold so slight she had to shift to feel his arms. His dark eyes remained steadfastly focused on the horizon beyond the trees, his gaze shifting back and forth as he scanned their surroundings.

A snowflake danced before her face. Another flew by. The wind kicked up as the snowfall increased, sending swirls of white spinning amid the dark greenery of the forest. She stuck her tongue out, catching a few on the tip.

Robert chuckled.

"What? You doona ever have fun?" she asked.

Robert pulled his arms away, and she turned around. He settled against the tree's scarred bark once again, folding his hands behind his lower back and propping the heel of a boot flat on the trunk. His gaze drifted beyond her and out of focus. "Aye, I have a bit of fun when time allows."

"What do you do for fun?" she asked.

Robert dropped a smoldering gaze to her. "Besides takin' what pleasures women offer me?" An unreadable emotion flashed across his face after the scandalous intimation, but then instantly disappeared, his eyes narrowing.

Her cheeks flushed hot. "Aye, besides that."

"Weel . . . I do love to hunt," he said.

"You're not huntin' now. 'Tis because I'm here?" she asked.

He tilted his head, the corners of his mouth twitching. "Not all prey are four-legged." He winked at her.

She laughed, shaking her head.

"Och, lass. You're verra bonnie when you smile."

Uncomfortable with his flattery, she lowered her gaze and unexpectedly caught the glint of an object. In the cuff of his boot was the hilt of a dagger.

Her dagger.

The smile fell from her face as her gaze drifted back up, assessing the striking man before her. Charming.

Devastating. *Enemy.*

"I'll remember to keep my smile to myself then."

A thunderous sound startled her, and she spun around to the loud cracks of snapping limbs, her heart racing. Thick scrub beneath the tree canopy shook, and a large stag broke into the clearing, stumbled, and fell, an arrow protruding behind its shoulder. Duncan and Seamus appeared through the brush, both men grinning and breathing heavily. Seamus stopped, squatted by the deer, and unsheathed a large blade from his thigh.

Robert brushed past her and met Duncan halfway into their small clearing. "I recall our deer park being a good distance away."

Duncan's grin widened. "Aye. Why not flush them your way, save us the long haul, and enjoy the sport of the kill?"

Robert chuckled, clapping a hand on his shoulder. "Duncan, you shall make a great commander."

While Seamus finished with the deer, the snowfall increased, tiny specks of white dusting down through openings in the canopy. Susanna occupied herself as best she could while waiting; sitting upon the stump of a tree, pacing the length of the clearing, and finally settling back against the alligatored bark of the pine beside Robert, where he'd calmly leaned the entire time.

With the passing minutes, she grew more restless. Not only did the looming danger of being apprehended weigh heavy on her thoughts, time spent around men in their natural element, without any purpose to occupy her hands or her mind, made her uneasy.

As Seamus strapped their bound kill to one of the horses, Duncan gravitated to the edge of the forest, staring out in the direction from where they'd come. Seamus soon joined him. Both men tensed, their hands hovering over the hilts of their swords.

Robert moved close behind her, his amazing heat penetrating through her cloak and dress. "Do you feel it?"

"Feel what?" she asked.

"Close your eyes, lass. Somethin' comes our way." Robert took a step ahead of her, physically shielding her from whatever approached.

She closed her eyes, uncertain what he meant. Cold flakes of snow hit her cheeks, but a distinct heat weighed heavy in the pit of her stomach. An ember deep inside glowed hotter, and she clutched at her belly.

Susanna recognized the sensation, only she'd never felt it from a great distance before. The wind carried a message only those attuned to the vibration could hear . . . and they all understood its meaning.

"My father," she whispered.

Robert had been right about something coming, and yet, a force greater than any of the men realized was at work. More than a simple feeling reverberated through her belly and seeped into her bones. Susanna opened her eyes. On the horizon, from a thick mist that hovered low to the ground, dark figures emerged. But they faded from her awareness as an epiphany sharpened into focus.

She'd escaped a threatening past, seeking to seize a secure future, but among three warriors who'd vowed to protect her—even against her tenacious will—every part of her snapped to life. Her perception had twisted from total independence to *oneness . . . with others.*

A surprising inner warrior emerged. She moved from behind Robert and stood tall beside him. Unarmed, yet unafraid for the first time since Robert had captured her, they now shared a common goal.

"All I feel is an enemy's arrogance." She kept her eyes trained on the growing shapes that galloped toward them. "However, I feel far less welcomin' to their breach of your clan lands than you were to me."

Robert glanced at her. "Ah, lass, you've no idea how pleased I am to hear those words."

Power emanated outward from Duncan and Seamus, from Robert . . . and from her. A trio of warriors and a petite woman stood strong against an unpredictable and obsessed enemy.

Susanna had never felt more secure.

Chapter Five

Brodie Castle—Thirteenth Century

Isobel struggled with the heavy oak chair, puffing an unruly lock of hair out of her face. With the toe of her favorite Brooks Brothers calfskin boots, she literally shooed away the growling wolfhound that staked his territory. The ornery beast gave her another inch. She took two with a final shove, making him move. Breathless, she leaned over the back of the chair, pleased that she'd made headway with the hearth's sitting area . . . and the dogs.

"Isa!" The growled shout of her name echoed through the great hall.

She smiled, looking up at her beloved Iain. Flames from the hearth glinted off strands of copper in his dark-brown hair, but it was his hazel eyes that sparked with fire.

"I strictly forbid you to move the furniture!"

She smiled at his stern expression and stood, wrapping her arms around his neck and kissing him passionately. His severe countenance softened under the assault of her lips, and she nipped at the corners of his mouth with playful butterfly kisses.

"You *strictly* forbid?" she teased. "You *know* I want to bring Christmas here. If you won't help, I'll do it myself," she said.

"Not at the risk of my bairns, you won't." He moved his

hands forward and cradled her swollen belly. "Doona test me further, Isa. I'll chain you if you push me."

Mischievous thoughts flickered through her mind. "Promise?"

Iain growled and smacked her ass. "Behave, woman."

Isobel planted her hands on her hips and lifted her chin, arching her brows in stubbornness. Iain knew well from repeated experience, his woman did not take kindly to orders. *Or restrictions . . .*

Iain stared at her for exactly fifteen seconds—she counted. On a labored sigh, he relented, the last of the angry furrows in his forehead relaxing. "Where would you like the chairs?"

She smiled triumphantly. That rumbling deep voice in his tantalizing brogue never failed to melt her heart.

She puffed the wavy lock from her lips again, but tucked it behind her ear when it failed to obey. "Over in a tighter arrangement to one side of the hearth." She pointed to the area she had in mind. "Robert promised to bring me back a tree, and I want there to be plenty of room."

Iain hoisted the mammoth carved oak chairs off the ground like they were nothing more than inflated beach balls. Powerful forearms flexed and released beneath the rolled cuffs of his linen shirt as she pointed and he placed, positioning them into an open but intimate sitting area for easy conversation.

"Robert's bringin' you a tree? Why not Uilleam? He's our woodcutter."

She hesitated, weighing Iain's inevitable reaction to her disobedience. Evasion tactics always failed with him, and she refused to lie, so she took a slow, deep breath, hoping to soften the blow with reasoning before admitting her transgression. "Iain, you *know* the personal nature of a Christmas tree, and our clan has never had one before. *We've* never had one. It had to be just right. So . . . I scouted one out." She sucked in another deep breath, desperate for oxygen in her baby-cramped lungs after blurting out her explanation all at once.

Iain froze in place, his back to her. He held the last of the two-ton chairs in midair, looking as if Michelangelo had carved an ad for a medieval furniture store.

Two seconds . . . three . . . four . . .

He lowered the final chair beside the other three, creating the conversation area she'd been envisioning. She didn't need him to turn around for her to know how he felt; he broadcasted his anger in the tense movement of his body.

His voice lowered and purred out smooth as silk, easily heard above the soft hum of the fire. "You went out without an escort?"

She had no desire to rile his barely restrained beast further, so replied quietly, "Yes."

"Please tell me you dinna mount *Solus*."

She took a tentative step closer to him. There was more than anger in his voice; an undercurrent of pain laced his tone. Her selfish wishes had hurt her great warrior, and she regretted her foolish actions.

"I'm sorry, my love. I did. I forced the stable boy to help me onto her with a stool, and I only rode her at a slow walk. At the time it seemed . . . adventurous. You'd battle-trained *Solus* so well, I had confidence she'd keep me safe."

Iain finally turned. The burgundy flecks in those hazel eyes flashed hot with passion: a mixture of fury, pain, and love. "Even our best horses—even *Dubhar*—can take a misstep. Do you think I demand anythin' from you lightly?"

Isobel dropped her gaze to his chest, unable to bear the tortured look in his eyes. She shook her head slowly.

He folded her into his arms and pulled her as close as her protruding belly would allow. "The verra wild spirit that I love in you must be tamed. You've put more at risk than the woman who I live and breathe for every day. Those bairns are the future of our clan. Their safety is paramount to your needs or mine, and my role as laird requires me to protect them. Do you understand what I'm sayin'?"

She stared into the crackling fire, realizing what she'd inadvertently done. When she'd gone off on a gentle ride on a crisp blue-sky day of momentary freedom, she'd guaranteed it would be the last time for a while.

"Yes, Iain. The escort you told me to request whenever I

left the keep will no longer be by request, will it?"

The solid chest that her cheek rested against shook, startling her. She lapsed into confusion by his low chuckle and looked up to see mirth in his eyes.

"Nay. You'll no longer even move *about this keep* without an escort."

Her jaw dropped with her brows. "What?" Shocked, she pushed against him hard. Iain released his hold, and she stumbled two steps backward for balance. He crossed his arms, all amusement vanishing from his face.

"No way." She also crossed her arms . . . onto the shelf that had become her belly.

"Oh, aye." He lowered his face, a determined stare locking onto her hers as he casually widened his stance.

They stood there for long moments, nostrils flaring, hearts thundering, each in defiance of the other's position: two stubborn souls brought together from different worlds— her twenty-first century to his thirteenth. The battle lines had been drawn. She snorted. If she wouldn't have to pee within the next thirty minutes, she'd have the stamina to stand there all day.

While she debated the odds of Iain granting any leeway if she begged for mercy, Brigid flew down the stairs and into the room in an epic huff. Her copper curls flew behind her as she stormed up and barged in between them, her own arms crossed over her chest. "I am *done* with that damned angel!"

Iain's gaze snapped to Brigid so fast, Isobel was certain he'd caused himself whiplash.

"*What* did you say?" Iain's growl trumped Brigid's. He stepped closer, glaring at her.

Unafraid of her brother, Brigid shot a frosty glare his way. "Done."

"The rest of it." Iain's voice had gone glacial as he towered over his sister.

Her voice lowered, but didn't cool. Brigid had endured a lifetime of Iain's intimidation tactics. "With. That. *Damned.* Angel." Brigid arched a brow.

"I hadn't been aware you'd been *with* that damned angel." Iain raised his brows.

He waited.

She relented on a sigh. "Aye, Iain, you have. You know Skorpius had been bound to protect me. Weel, I've been gone a while, you've been busy with the clan, and 'tis a verra long story." She arched a defiant brow at him. "I'll share it when I'm ready."

Unfortunately, Brigid's keen observation skills had failed to take into account the hostility of the party she'd joined. A slow smile spread across Iain's face as he backed up, his gaze sliding toward Isobel then back again to look at his sister. Finally, he spoke, addressing Isobel without taking his eyes off his sister. "*Brigid.* She will now go with you everywhere you go. Brigid, *you* are not to leave Isa's side."

Brigid opened her mouth in a sure attempt at protest, but her words were left unspoken as Iain growled low in warning.

"I doona care if you have to lift each other's skirts in the garderobe. Each of you will be *everywhere* with the other. If you both leave this keep" —he paused and glared at Isobel— "and I mean *one step off this wooden floor out the door*, you will do so with the escort of one of my guard. Do I make myself clear?"

Isobel withheld comment. So did Brigid. Too late, Isobel realized their lack of response was a monumental mistake on both of their stubborn parts; they apparently liked to poke a riled bear.

Iain's face turned crimson with anger until he looked ready to explode in volcanic eruption. Instead, he took a deep breath, the harsh color fading from his face. His voice dropped to a dead calm laced with venom. "Do I make myself clear, Isobel?"

He never used her formal name. She'd infuriated him before, but not to this level. Needing to soothe the riot she'd incited in her man, she restrained her inner feistiness. "Yes, Iain. I understand."

Brigid shot a surprised look her way, but wisely mimicked Isobel's statement. "Yes, Iain. I understand."

"Good. I'm done with both of your flagrant acts of disobedience and your hidin' them from me. When you deign to obey the rules I set for you and the clan for your own safety, you'll get more lenience from me. Doona disappoint me again. Either of you."

The two women watched in silence as Iain stormed from the great hall, the heavy oak front door slamming shut on its iron hinges. They both loved Iain dearly, and his overbearing protection did help balance their unchecked mischief.

Isobel put her hands on her hips and stared in sheer disbelief at her new *everywhere* companion. "That damned angel? You can't mean . . . *Cupcake.*"

Brigid half-rolled her eyes, stopping and staring at the ceiling. On a long sigh, her friend's gaze dropped down to meet hers. "'Tis a *verra verra* long story."

Chapter Six

Robert looked forward to a confrontation with Susanna's father, but as the small party came into sight across the vast meadow of snow, he realized the chance of her father being among them was slight. And that thought disappointed him.

He'd heard MacEalan was ruthless. Broc had formed alliances with clans that had risen against the Brodie, which made him an enemy. The fact that the vibrant creature beside him had fled from him—*had been willing to kill for her freedom*—made him eager to do battle with the tyrant. The very notion that something horrible might've happened to her at his hands made him want to kill the man.

"I still doona understand why we had to wait," Susanna grumbled.

She'd grown more and more agitated all afternoon, pacing almost nonstop. The woman had homed in on her instincts; her body and soul sensing the impending danger as it approached long before her mind did. Unfortunately, nothing in Robert's power enabled him to lessen the impact of her fears.

"We wait because we must. 'Tis our only way home," he replied.

She scowled at him, catapulted her icy glare at the approaching party, and then turned, heading toward the tree where they'd been sheltered most of the day.

Robert let her have a moment to herself as he walked

over to Seamus and Duncan. The men were on edge. Years of training and hundreds of fights had prepared them for any encounter, and they tasted the same aggression in the air he did.

"You two remain here. Whatever comes, it pursues Susanna. We protect her first." Robert gathered the reins of their horses.

"We are yours, Commander," Seamus said, staring in the direction of their approaching enemy for another heartbeat before striding over to his horse. With calm efficiency, he pulled the axes from their packs and tossed Duncan one.

Once the men had what they needed, Robert led the horses toward Susanna, sheltering the animals from harm, planning to use them in defense if necessary. The fierce wind had calmed, but the snow continued, fat flakes drifting down one after another. Susanna shivered as the sun crept lower, robbing the waning afternoon of its scant warmth.

Robert stepped in front of her and wrapped his hands around her upper arms, rubbing them. He glanced down at her. "Those men will not harm you."

Her gaze locked onto the horizon beyond Duncan and Seamus. "I'll gain my freedom, or die tryin'."

"You'll not die this night, lass," he said.

She exhaled a slow breath, but her demeanor told him the action came from determination, not frustration. Her entire stance had changed, becoming more rigid as she prepared herself like they all did. A twinge of pride jolted through his chest at her display of courage.

The approaching party grew closer, dark shapes bobbing amid a field of pristine white. Robert counted just over half a dozen men and snorted. Two to one was nowhere near fair, but not every fight promised great challenge.

None wore a clan plaid, but that didn't surprise him. Plaids were only recently adopted as functional clothing by Iain's introduction of the pattern to Clan Brodie's wool. As was more customary, leather clad the riders' legs down to their boots, and fur covered their upper torsos. The leader of their party rode a horse whose bridle was decorated with elaborate precious-metal designs.

The group stopped just short of Duncan and Seamus, chunks of snow flying into the air as their horses' hooves dug into the ground. Predictably, not one of the men was Susanna's father, as none bore the purported jagged scar down his face.

"Do you recognize him?" Robert asked her.

The man bellowed. "I know you have her. Surrender the wee whore to us, and we won't cause bloodshed."

"Dougal. He's the man my father"—she shuddered—"sold me to. He gave my father fertile land and gold and silver in exchange for my father forcin' me to be his . . . wife . . . but I dinna marry him."

"Susanna!" the man shouted, his frizzy matted locks shaking from his scalp. "You've caused me great embarrassment. For that you shall pay. Your father wanted to come after you. In fact, he took great pleasure in the thought. I insisted he remain behind, however, imaginin' you'd rather submit to my will than his."

Robert ignored the trespasser's rants, glancing at her. "Was there a treaty made?"

"Aye. I doona care. I'll not be like my mother. No woman should have to suffer the way she has."

Robert growled.

Dougal drew his sword, the ring of its metal the only battle cry the Brodie needed. Then Dougal kicked his horse, leading his animal wide and out of their sight while two of the men he'd brought urged their mounts the opposite direction and the other four directly charged their stand of trees.

Fools.

Seamus and Duncan moved apart in a blur.

Like water rushing over jagged rocks, Robert's men jumped and fell in response to each obstacle in their way. With Seamus's boulder of a fist, he unseated the first unlucky man from his horse and buried an ax deep into his heart right as his victim's back hit the ground. Duncan unsheathed his sword, ducked under an arcing blade, and sprung into the air, piercing a rider through one side and out the other.

As their commander and natural-born strategist, Robert held back from the immediate fray, his senses heightened to detect their unseen foe. His men continued in silent grace, deadly shadows moving amid pure, white snowfall, dispatching their enemy with unparalleled skill. Robert turned, keeping Susanna at his back, as he scanned for movement through the trees. He'd been hunted by a hungry predator before, including men wishing to end his life. Never had it been with a woman on the battlefield.

"Susanna, stay between my back and the horses."

"Aye, Robert. I've no intention of bein' anywhere else."

He nodded, pleased that she cooperated with him against their common enemy. Mental notes of the weapons Dougal possessed flashed through his mind as Robert unsheathed a claymore from a scabbard strapped to their spare horse.

Robert relegated unnecessary sounds into background noise as adrenaline spiked through his veins, honing his senses. With keen eyesight and hearing, he distinguished each move their attackers made: the shift in a saddle, a twig that broke beneath a hoof, snow that crunched on a dismount.

With slowing breaths, he closed his eyes and calmed the heartbeat pounding in his ears. On instinct, his body readied for the fight: weight shifted to the balls of his feet, muscles relaxed, charged awareness amplified. On an inhale, he opened his eyes, flexing his fingers one hand at a time on the leather hilt.

A dark shape flashed to his far left, and Robert spun around.

Susanna shifted behind him, quick as his shadow.

Disturbed air rippled to his right.

A flash of metal arced past his shoulder.

Susanna gasped.

He shot his claymore up, catching the descending smaller sword. The deafening ring of blade crashing into blade pierced his ears. Robert shoved a shoulder into the block, throwing his opponent backward. He jerked the hilt higher, punching a hard blow into the attacker's jaw.

Dougal grunted, stumbling back. "You've no right to

her," he growled, spitting out blood and adjusting a jaw that had likely been cracked.

Robert squinted at him. "You speak the truth. She seeks sanctuary here. You've no right to her either."

On a roar, Dougal charged forward, swinging his lighter, one-handed sword. Robert held his ground, unwilling to expose Susanna. Robert deflected the flying blade, but Dougal spun around at the last moment, arcing his sword under Robert's, slicing the razor edge into his side above a rib.

Susanna gasped.

Robert hissed, wincing at the pain, but remained focused on the danger. He had to get Susanna to safety. Duncan and Seamus must've given chase to the remaining two attackers, or they would've arrived to assist them.

Focusing on his opponent, Robert circled around in deliberate steps, his hands gripping the hilt only tight enough to direct his claymore without choking his ability for fluid movement. Susanna moved in graceful motion with him. He caught a slight hesitation in Dougal's rhythm and shifted his weight into his leading hip, arcing his weapon wide and low.

He caught a flash of movement down behind him, but concentrated all his energy forward, following through on the forceful swing. Blade met blade with a loud *clang* that reverberated through Robert's arm and into his entire body, but the crushing force of the impact sheared his opponent's sword in half. Both men blinked, shocked at the improbable occurrence. Robert slowly lowered his newer claymore, staring at it, wondering if Iain had the smithy weave magick into its metal or if Dougal's blade had an inherent flaw.

A sudden whir of air brushed by Robert's ear as a dagger flew past his face, straight and true. The blade embedded into Dougal's left upper chest up to its jeweled hilt. Dougal gaped down wide-eyed. A moment later, he coughed up blood.

Robert inhaled a deep breath, realizing what Susanna had done. Not only had she thrown her weapon expertly, she'd pierced Dougal's lung.

In the few seconds it took for the two men to recalculate

their odds of victory, Robert felt the heavy presence of his formidable clansmen descend among them—the air sizzled with immense power. Without turning around, he slowly smiled at the hunched-over Dougal, whose chances had just vanished in a wisp of smoke.

"This isna over," Dougal threatened, another bloodied cough sputtering out.

The vegetation to Robert's immediate left rustled, and he spun toward the sound, reaching back and wrapping an arm around Susanna as he guided her in step with him. A scuffle broke through the low brush, and Seamus and Duncan burst into the small clearing, engaged in hand-to-hand combat with two of Dougal's men.

Robert snapped his attention back toward Dougal at the instant the injured man was being hoisted onto a horse by one of Dougal's soldiers. Once Dougal was seated behind the man, the horse galloped off into the forest, vanishing from sight.

Instinct bunched his muscles, readying him to chase the enemy down; however, he forced a grounding breath into his lungs, nostrils flaring. Vengeance would have to wait a little longer. When he granted Dougal the bloody death he deserved, it would be far easier on Susanna if she didn't witness the gruesome event

With the need to protect Susanna pumping hard through his veins, he turned around to find her shaking from head to toe. Her face was red, tightened into an enraged scowl. Her chest heaved as she stared off into the darkened forest where Dougal had fled.

"Susanna?"

Her gaze remained unfocused beyond his shoulder. She'd gone far away, somewhere else entirely.

He cupped a hand over her cheek. "Susanna. Lass, come back."

She blinked a few times and shifted her gaze up to his. Those striking blue eyes sparked with fury. Her mouth opened, but no words came out. She closed it on a hard swallow.

"Thank you, lass. You've a fierce protectiveness in you

that I admire. You've great aim, as well, as good as any of my men." He winked at her, attempting to pull her from her dark shock.

She took in a deep breath and exhaled slowly. "I want him to suffer. To remember. To know what it's like to be deeply scarred."

He chuckled. "Aye. I'll wager he'll never forget." In fact, he soon planned to remind Dougal in painstaking detail before delivering the ultimate parting message on Susanna's behalf.

"He has my dagger," she grumbled.

"Did it serve the purpose you'd intended?"

The corners of her mouth twitched, a glint flashing in her eye. "Aye."

"The dagger can be replaced. 'Tis a lesson to him that a human is not to be taken against their will. *In any manner.*"

"Aye, I'm glad he has the dagger. 'Twill be the only piece of me he'll ever have."

He smiled down at her, both in pride of what she'd done and in admiration of the strength she'd found inside herself. She'd need that fortitude until he dealt properly with Dougal, for until her tormenter was forcefully removed from this world, she would feel hunted.

Another frisson of energy sizzled into Robert's awareness, and he finally glanced up at the impressive force that had come out to greet them. Clan Brodie and her castle had finally arrived. They waited no longer.

"Susanna, turn around. 'Tis time to go home."

Chapter Seven

Susanna turned around, and her jaw dropped as she registered an imposing army of men standing just beyond the tree line. She blinked hard, twice, for she swore one of the men—a good head taller than the rest—had enormous black ... *wings?* Beyond the men, further up the rise, rose a formidable stone wall and the turrets of a castle that disappeared into a dark-clouded sky—*a castle which hadn't been there before.*

Fragile snowflakes continued to drift down while she stared in silent wonder at the unbelievable sight. Had the snowfall been so heavy she hadn't noticed a castle through the trees? She shook her head. From the time she was knee-high, she'd always thoroughly scanned her surroundings, everywhere she went. Doing so helped identify danger and had protected her on many occasions.

"That is your clan's castle?" she asked, unable to clarify her confusion.

"Aye, lass. She's remarkable, is she not?"

"Aye. I seem to be in dire need of food, however. My hunger has affected my senses." She raised her hand to her forehead, covering her right eye and peered at the extraordinary sight, including the winged man, with her uncovered left.

Robert laughed. "Of course, lass. Are you ill?"

"Perhaps," she replied, lifting the fingers of both hands

to her temples. "I doona know if I hit my head yesterday, or if I've gone too long without eatin' today, but I'm seein' things that are not there and failin' to notice things that are."

From behind, Robert wrapped his arms around her. They were solid, comforting. In her internal distress, she welcomed an embrace that she would've shunned a few short hours ago.

The one with wings—massive, glistening black wings that arched two feet higher than his shoulders—vanished before her eyes. Amazed, and certain she hadn't blinked, she closed her eyelids heavily and reopened them to find the creature still missing.

Robert dropped his mouth to her ear, sending a shiver down her spine. "Lass, you shall enjoy a sumptuous feast. Then we'll talk of all the things you saw and failed to see."

She nodded absently. An army whose collective gaze had rested on her disbursed upon seeing Robert's arms wrapped around her in evident claim. With her hands gripping the muscular forearms that bound her waist, she welcomed his protection . . . for the moment.

On foot, Duncan and Seamus led their horses, including the one carrying the stag they'd killed and another towing the pine tree they'd harvested. Robert ushered her behind them, over a wooden drawbridge spanning an icy moat, his right arm wrapped around her shoulders.

She caught sight of him pressing his left hand to his side, his fingers covered in fresh blood. "Robert! You're hurt!" She tried to turn to better assess his injury.

Robert's right hand gripped her shoulder, preventing her escape from his hold. "Nay, love. 'Tis but a scratch. Doona worry over me."

She huffed out a white puff of air as their boots echoed over the last wooden planks of the drawbridge. Amid a list of things out of her control since she'd escaped her father's domain, the most bewildering of all was that Robert had just called her love. No one but Mama had uttered the endearment to Susanna, and her chest seized with sudden upset. She took in short, deep breaths, scanning the castle grounds as she tried to calm herself.

An astonishing scene unfolded in the castle's great

courtyard, scattering the troubles that whirled in her head. She paused, watching in surprise as merriment abounded everywhere she looked. At least half a dozen children chased a large wolfhound puppy, the dog and the children sliding in the new-fallen snow. Squeals of laughter rang out while everyone scrambled up and chased one another again.

A large warrior stalked up behind the children and launched a huge ball of snow from his fist. The wet clump splattered onto the shoulder of one of the children, sticking to the child's dark woolen cape.

The young boy spun around. "Laird!" All the boy's companions sprang into action, scooping up snow and launching it at their laird and each other.

She stared in rapt fascination.

Robert laughed, his face dropping near her ear. "That would be Laird Iain. The closer fatherhood comes to the man, the more he plays among the wee ones."

Fresh snowballs were thrown from every direction as a crowd gathered at a safe perimeter to watch the fun. A few other men and many more children joined in the frosty battle.

"Listen to them, Robert," she whispered, amazed. "Listen to all the laughter."

"Aye." Robert squeezed her arm, a broad smile on his face. "Come, Susanna. 'Tis cold, and we're both tired. Let's get inside to soak in hot baths."

"A hot bath? Truly?" She gaped at him, shocked such a luxury would be extended to a stranger.

"Aye. I'd wager there's one already bein' drawn for you."

She stared in disbelief, yet he guided her forward, urging them toward the sizable keep. The hill they climbed was gradual, but two feet of snow on the ground made her steps heavier than normal, and she soon labored for breath, hot puffs of fog flowing out from her lips.

Dozens of steep-roofed cottages had been frosted in white, their blackened stacks spiraling out a thin tendril of dark smoke. Two soldiers on horseback rode by to their left and continued down to larger structures, where they dismounted before the open doors of a stable.

Duncan and Seamus untied the pine tree, and Seamus hoisted it upon one of his massive shoulders before heading their same direction. As their group approached a great oak door through a stone archway, Duncan jogged ahead of them and pushed it open. Robert held Susanna back as Seamus squeezed backward through the doorway with the tree, its branches scraping either side of the wooden frame.

The bittersweet scent of pine filled her nostrils as they stepped into a great hall unlike her wildest imaginings; her view of the glittering scene opened wide as Seamus veered off toward a massive stone hearth.

Short, fat beeswax candles on a multitude of ledges gleamed with orange flame while slender tapers flickered in ornate, multi-pronged frames in the corners of the gigantic room. Fresh rushes and a purple haze of dried lavender covered the expansive oak floor. Long lengths of greenery were stretched across wooden tables beside red bows and branches of white berries gathered into piles. Attendants moved about the room carrying one decorative thing or another as a flurry of activity happened everywhere Susanna looked.

"Seamus!" an attractive, very pregnant woman with wavy blond hair shouted. "You're dropping snow from that tree with each step you take."

Seamus paused midgait without looking over to her. He tightened the fist that engulfed the trunk of the tree and rapidly shook his forearm. With the force of the sudden tremors, the remaining snow from every last pine needle quivered off, raining onto the floor where he stood.

"There, M'Lady. My pardon for mussin' your hall," Seamus said with a smirk. His next steps were snowfall free.

The woman rolled her eyes and kept them toward the ceiling, muttering something about the Lord ... and patience. Susanna followed the woman's gaze upward to see dramatic stone beams that arched toward the center of the cavernous room. Their remarkable bluish gray surface sparkled in the firelight.

She dropped her gaze back down at Robert's gentle tug.

"M'Lady, this is Susanna. I hope to provide her refuge

here. Perhaps a hot bath and a hearty meal to start," Robert said.

Susanna looked into two brilliant emerald eyes. Tiny dimples appeared on the woman's cheeks as she grinned broadly. "It's very nice to meet you, Susanna. Please call me Isobel."

Susanna gasped as her jaw dropped and remained open. She snapped it shut upon the realization. "You're English?"

"Yes," Isobel replied.

"I'm English, too!" Susanna cringed the moment the blurted words burned her ears. Several heads turned their way. Her cheeks flamed hot at the sudden realization of what she'd admitted, which was only a half-truth.

Isobel cocked her head and opened her mouth, like she was about to say something.

Robert interrupted, turning to Susanna. "You're English? You doona *sound* English."

Susanna glanced up at Robert, her heart racing. With the damage already done, she promptly explained. "My mother was from England."

Surprisingly, Robert's expression softened, and he nodded, as if a missing puzzle piece had been placed. An odd relief washed through her at his lack of judgment.

Distracted by having something in common with another soul, she shifted her attention back to Isobel. "Mama told me countless stories about England, sharin' many things she missed greatly about her country."

Isobel smiled weakly. "Uhhh ... I come from a place of the English also—but not from your mother's England." Isobel's gaze locked with Robert's for a brief instant. "We'll talk more about that later, though. Let's get you into a hot bath."

Another young woman, Susanna guessed Isobel's sister, stepped forward. "Hello, Susanna. I'm Brigid. I'll take her up, Isobel."

Isobel sighed. "Not alone. I'm coming with. Iain will be back any moment, and I don't need to catch a lecture or worse for straying one moment from your side."

Brigid took Susanna's hand and led her to the wide stone

steps that lined the front wall. A gentle tug from Brigid made her pause as they waited for Isobel to start her slow ascent. Susanna watched as the woman in a soft-gray day dress took each step with poised grace, leaning one delicate hand on the wall for balance.

Isobel suddenly yelled out without turning around, "Robert, go straight to the apothecary before one more drop of your blood hits the floor."

Robert's laughter rumbled out behind them. "Aye, M'Lady."

Once they reached the landing, Susanna was led down a hall, past several closed doors, to a room whose entrance stood at an angle in the hall's bend. Brigid grasped the decorative iron handle and pushed. The sound of creaking hinges tickled into Susanna's ears as they entered a spacious, bright bedchamber.

A maid stood over a sizable wooden barrel in the center of the room, pouring steaming water into the tub from a large pitcher. Another maid arranged garments on the bed: a chemise, a ruby gown, and a hair comb adorned with emeralds. Matching ruby slippers were deposited on the wooden floor.

"Would you like to bathe alone, or would you prefer our company?" Isobel asked.

Susanna blinked. No one had seen her unclothed body before, besides Mama.

She'd also never had any contact with other females her age; she'd never been allowed a single friend. And no one but Mama had extended any courtesy or kindness to her. In her dark and sheltered world, no one had been given the chance.

"I'd . . . like company, if that's acceptable," she said in a soft tone. As unnerving as it was to bare herself before others, she was more afraid to be left alone in a castle full of strangers.

Isobel nodded to both of the maids. They gave a polite nod in return and quietly left the room.

Susanna bent over, untied the laces to her worn leather boots, and stepped out of them. Weary from the day, she slowly reached leaden arms behind her back to undress.

"Allow me to help," Brigid said. She circled behind and tugged at the ribbons tied at the back of Susanna's gown. The dress was one of her mother's—a gown she cherished, since Mama had often told her that its rich sapphire hue matched her eyes in the firelight.

Susanna held the bodice over her breasts as the material fell free. Bashful in front of the two women, she stood facing away from them as they helped her lift the gown and chemise over her head.

Cool air from the room danced over her skin, cascading goose bumps over arms and chest before she stepped into the tub. With one hand gripped on the wooden rim and the other holding Brigid's hand, she gingerly lowered herself into the hot water.

She groaned, closing her eyes as soothing heat penetrated aching muscles, some of which she hadn't realized were sore and others she hadn't known she possessed. Although she'd snuck out on many an occasion to learn how to ride a horse, she'd never ridden longer than a stolen hour on any given day over the last few summers. Hours upon hours for a day and a half on horseback had taken a toll on her body she hadn't anticipated. Knowing the result, however, wouldn't have made any difference in her choice to escape. The price was small compared to the alternative.

Isobel's soft voice interrupted her thoughts. "Lavender soaps are beside you on the table, Susanna."

She opened her eyes to see Isobel waddling over to a wooden chair on the other side of the table. Brigid had grabbed the arms of another chair, and its legs scraped across the floor as she dragged it beside Isobel's.

Once Isobel finally reached her chair, she turned, gripped its arms with her hands, and lowered her body down onto the seat. She moaned softly and closed her eyes, relaxing back against a black velvet, rectangular pillow with gold-braided edges and tasseled corners.

Susanna let out a soft laugh. Apparently, life had been rough for more than just herself.

Isobel opened a single eye and peered at her, snorting with a smirk on her face. "Iain forbids me to *strain* myself in my condition. I'll not let that man govern my every finger lift and step. But on occasion, I'm grateful to take a much needed break and rest."

Isobel dropped her head a degree and squinted at Brigid before she directed a severe look at Susanna. "Don't either of you dare breathe a word of that to Iain." She winked at Susanna.

"Och!" Brigid said. "I'd no sooner give information to my brother than he'd give it to me."

"Amen, sister," Isobel said.

Both women laughed with unguarded abandon, and their light-hearted banter amazed Susanna. A jovial bond between two women was something she'd never experienced before—and immediately loved.

Susanna dipped a linen square beneath the steaming water and brought it up, rubbing the lavender-scented soap into the material as she enjoyed another luxury she'd never had before. After a cloud of fragrant suds formed, she ran the decadent cloth from her wrist up her arm to her shoulder, pressing hard in a long stroke. A thousand muscles slowly relaxed, including her mind. She failed to remember a time when she had no cares, when she and Mama hadn't worried about the very next minute . . . each minute of their lives.

The peace and safety of Isobel and Brigid's home, the happiness abounding everywhere—the love evident in the hearts of the people she'd encountered—ran directly against everything she'd been taught. It opposed everything she believed about the world.

All men are *bad. They're at the root of every woman's sorrow.*

Susanna exhaled, lowering the cloth beneath the surface as she cleaned the rest of her body. She decided to worry about the greater world later, opting to enjoy this glimpse of happiness God had granted.

She cupped water into her hands and tried to wet her hair, but more splashed outside the tub than within.

Brigid laughed. "Doona drown us. Relax. I'll help."

Her volunteer bath attendant crossed the room, fetched a ceramic pitcher off a far table, and gripped the vessel with one hand on the handle and the other cradled beneath as she carried it over.

"Why are you both bein' so kind to me?" Susanna bit her lip the moment she inadvertently voiced the candid question.

Brigid rested the water pitcher on the lip of the tub and looked down at her, tilting her head. "I doona know any other way to be to someone in need of a friend." She glanced up at Isobel. "On a rare occasion, a person comes into your life and you doona know how or why, but you *know* them. You feel connected in ways you canna explain. I never question the uncommon gifts of friendship and love—I embrace them."

Isobel smiled. "Brigid, you are a generous soul. Were it not for you, who knows what would've happened to me." She glanced at Susanna. "We're here to support you. It's not easy being thrust into an unfamiliar situation. Trust me. I *so* know about being a stranger in a foreign land. Relying on the strength of the people around you will help you discover the same within yourself."

"Close your eyes," Brigid said.

Susanna began to process what Isobel had said as she closed her eyes. An unexpected rush of warm water flowed over her head and face, and she sputtered as it splashed into her nose and mouth. She laughed, wiping her face with a hand.

Brigid took the soap from her, dunked her hands in the water, and rubbed them together, creating a thick lather. She dropped the soap into the tub and buried her hands into Susanna's hair, pulling the locks up into a heap atop her head and rubbing her scalp with firm fingers.

Relaxed by Brigid's massage, Susanna sighed and settled back against the tub.

"Susanna, where are you from?" Brigid asked.

The muscles in Susanna's back stiffened, a line of instant tension shooting from her spine into her shoulders. Unable to stop the sudden emotional reaction, her heart raced like a rabbit's.

"Shhh . . . 'tis fine, Susanna. No one cares if you doona tell us. I dinna mean to pry." Brigid urged her back against the tub with gentle pressure until she relaxed once again.

"Hmmm . . ." hummed Isobel while keeping her eyes shut. "You're very curious when it comes to others, but you and your brother are the best secret keepers I know, when it suits your amusement."

"Or need," Brigid huffed. "Some details are shared only when the time is right."

Isobel opened one eye again, arching her brow as she peered at Brigid. "Funny how need is subjective—viewed differently from the *secret keeper* and the one who would most benefit from said secret."

Brigid's tone softened. "Close your eyes again, Susanna."

She did as instructed and held her breath as warm water flowed over her head. A second pour came down, streaming back and forth over both sides of her face.

"You're no worse for wear, Isobel. You've become happy as a fat cat now," Brigid said.

"Hey! Watch the fat commentary, or I promise to be merciless when it's your turn to be with child," Isobel said.

Brigid snorted. "Go ahead and stand, Susanna. I've a wee bit of water left to rinse, if you'd like."

Susanna stood in the tub while reflecting on the playful teasing between the two close friends—on what Isobel had said about relying on the kindness and strength of others—and she began to believe in the tempting promise of the unanticipated notion. She still found the thought of trusting strangers difficult to grasp with everything that a lifetime of self-preservation had ingrained in her. But for whatever short time she had with the two compassionate women, she wanted to be a part of their special connection in whatever small way she was granted.

While Brigid poured the last of the water in the pitcher over her body, Susanna took a deep breath, readying to pour her heart out to her new friends. "I'm the daughter of Broc MacEalan. I've run away, and I'm never goin' back," she blurted.

Isobel's eyes popped open, but no other muscle in her body moved; she remained slouched in the chair. Brigid wrapped a warm linen towel around her from behind. Neither woman uttered a word in reply to her outburst.

Susanna took a second deep breath as her nerves calmed by a minute degree. "They dinna treat women right there, especially Mama. Laird Broc ripped her from the arms of her father in England, when she was just sixteen summers . . . against her will. By the time he removed her bindings and set her free to walk around, she'd become a prisoner in his castle."

Brigid gasped.

Isobel's hand flew over her mouth. She lowered her fingers to her chin, whispering, "Did she try to escape, to return back to England?"

"Nay," Susanna replied. "Broc learned how much her family meant to her and used it against her. He promised that if she ever tried to run away, it would matter not whether she succeeded. He would send his men to kill her papa, her mama, and all of her five younger brothers and sisters. Because she loved her family, she gave him her word that she would never attempt escape. She never did."

Susanna stepped out from the tub with the towel wrapped around her and turned to face them. Her friends' faces were furrowed with pain and concern.

"After he repeatedly . . . *raped* . . . her, I soon took shape in her belly. I've grown up in that castle as a prisoner in my own home. Mama and I have been subjected to his cruel barbs, and she's suffered his physical mistreatment. 'Tis all I've known."

"Oh, you poor thing." Isobel stood from the chair with a grunt and some effort. She walked over and enfolded Susanna in the best hug her swollen belly would allow. Brigid wrapped them both in her arms.

Susanna closed her eyes and just . . . *breathed*. Something as simple as comfort from two strangers, who'd become trusted friends in the span of a soul-baring bath, washed over her like a healing balm.

Isobel broke their tight embrace and grasped Susanna's shoulders, staring at her with a hardened expression. "Enough talk of the past. We need to get you fed, and I've a decorating party to orchestrate." She winked at Brigid. "Ready to eat well and have some fun, Susanna?"

Susanna's mouth fell open, her brain struggling to process all of Isobel's words. *Fun* hung in the air like a glittering dust mote caught in a moon beam. Delicate and elusive, she'd always hoped to capture such a treasure for more than a fleeting moment. Yet in a stranger's home, something that seemed but a fairy tale was being offered as if an everyday occurrence.

She inhaled, shifting her gaze between the two companions who still loosely held her. On a slow exhale, the memory of a random snowball fight filled her head, and she smiled.

"Aye. I'm verra ready to have some fun."

Chapter Eight

Were it not for the supportive arm of Brigid on her right and Isobel on her left, Susanna would've tumbled down the unforgiving stone steps straight to the bottom. Stuck in a fog of wonderment, she couldn't tear her gaze away from the bustling activity and festive adornment in their great hall.

Small candles in suspended glass jars flickered every few feet, appearing to float in the air. Greenery had been draped across the wide mantle high above the hearth, small red bows and white berries pinned within its lush branches. Two dozen people filled the room in comfortable groups of three or four, their animated conversations, and their laughter, drifting up to her ears.

Isobel briefly squeezed her forearm then tore away in haste, clutching the skirt of her emerald gown as she rushed down the steps. "Iain Brodie! Get that wolfhound away from the tree's water. It'll dry out!"

Iain turned from the men he'd been with, his dark hair glinting flashes of copper from all the firelight in the room. Isobel's husband was as formidable a man as Susanna had ever seen. A good bit taller and broader than her father, the fierceness in his eyes and the unmistakable power emanating from him broadcasted that he'd well earned his title as laird of their clan.

In spite of his daunting fearsomeness, a broad grin broke out on the man's face the moment his eyes met Isobel's.

Susanna's heart warmed at seeing something so rare between the young couple.

In garbled Gaelic, Iain issued a harsh command to the three beasts hovering near the iron base at the bottom of the tree. They flattened their ears and cowered away, curling up behind chairs on the far side of the hearth.

Iain directed an arched-brow look at one of their maids, and she disappeared. She returned moments later with a pitcher and poured its contents into the iron tree-holder. "Doona worry, my love. Your tree shall be cared for as if it was a treasured member of this family."

Isobel smiled and kissed Iain while he moved his flattened palms to either side of her belly. She raised her hands to his face, and any further words they spoke were lost to the rising buzz of resuming conversations.

Brigid tugged at Susanna's arm, leading her down the remaining steps. Susanna's gaze drifted across two long tables being set with a sumptuous feast. Her mouth watered as the tempting scents of cooked meat and freshly baked bread wafted beneath her nose.

She scanned left toward a sudden, compelling presence. A commanding man stared up at her, standing directly in their path with one boot propped upon the bottom step.

Robert.

At once, her breath caught and her heart fluttered. He looked spectacular . . . and intimidating. He'd donned a fresh plaid in his clan's dark green and black pattern and wore it perfectly pleated over a crisp linen shirt that set off his sun-bronzed skin. Long, black hair fell beyond his shoulders, a fresh braid at each temple shining in the light of the room. His dark brows drew together over those expressive dark-brown eyes.

His broad chest expanded as he inhaled a deep breath. "Susanna, you're a *stunnin'* sight."

A heated flush began beneath the low-cut neckline of her dress, where his gaze had fallen. In slow pace—as if he didn't want to miss a thing—he lifted his face until his intense stare met hers. She vaguely felt Brigid loosen her hold and slip away, the entire room vanishing with her.

All Susanna saw was the fearless warrior standing below, gazing up at her like he adored her.

Spellbound, as if caught in a haze of fairy dust, she descended the last two steps and slid her trembling hand across his outstretched palm. Warm. Solid.

"You look strikin' yourself, Highlander."

He tipped his head at her while she tried to define what was different about him, but she couldn't quite place it. Perhaps it was the way he carried himself or the tone in his voice. He seemed to have changed in some small way since she'd last seen him.

His familiar scent enveloped her, a unique woodsy fragrance that she hadn't clearly noticed until she'd been deprived of it. She inhaled the alluring spice and felt an odd peace, an inexplicable rightness.

"Come, Susanna. Let me introduce you to Iain before we eat."

With his warm hand placed firmly at her lower back, Robert led her toward where his laird and lady stood amid a small group. As they approached, Isobel's face lit up with a radiant smile the instant she caught sight of them.

Susanna smiled back, unable to hide the joyous feeling in her heart of having an unexpected first friendship. With each step, her budding confidence built.

Iain's gaze swung toward them as they neared, and he pinned an intense glare on Robert.

Isobel leaned toward her husband while still smiling at Susanna. "Iain, this is the guest Robert brought. Susanna, this is my husband, Iain."

Iain continued to hold Robert's gaze while the two women waited in silence. A muscle tensed in Iain's jaw. Susanna swallowed hard, beginning to feel uncomfortable as Robert's hand slid further around her, gripping her possessively.

Unfortunately, she was familiar with barely veiled hostility. As a child born into a world of hatred and contempt, she'd become acquainted with the mild form of aggression. The men carried on a silent conversation, and they didn't care if anyone else took notice. Iain's attention slowly shifted from Robert to her, but his expression didn't soften. Two piercing eyes stared at her, penetrating deep into her soul, as if seeking some response to a wordlessly bellowed question.

Her spine straightened of its own accord. Not once had she wilted under the threat or reality of men, and she had no intention of doing so now.

The corners of his lips twitched. "'Tis an honor to meet you, lass. Please, join us and enjoy the generous and unendin' hospitality of the Brodie."

Iain extended his arm, but Susanna caught sight of Isobel elbowing him in the ribs. The man held his posture, but inhaled deeply, as if challenged to restrain himself and not grunt.

Robert leaned down, whispering into her ear. "Doona mind him, Susanna. His temper flares with surprises. 'Twill be my issue to handle."

"'Tis unfortunate I'm an issue at all," she muttered then instantly bit her lower lip, shocked that she'd given words to her thoughts. "'Tis not because I'm half English, is it?"

Robert chuckled softly, nipping her earlobe. "Nay. *You* are not the issue. My reckless actions are. And I think he better enjoy havin' English lasses in his castle. His wife is one." His voice lowered into a rumbled growl. "I've taken a sudden interest in the English myself."

Blushing, she pulled her ear away from his scorching mouth and turned, glaring into dark mischievous eyes. "You should be careful what you take an interest in. The English are verra unpredictable."

He laughed louder and ushered her behind the thinning crowd as everyone found a place at the table. Iain sat at the head with a glowing Isobel beside him. Robert led Susanna to a place on the wooden bench next to Brigid, who sat on Iain's other side. An imposing man sat a little further down from Isobel, across from Robert. He was engaged in a heated debate with the soldier to his right. Susanna thought he bore a striking resemblance to their laird; even from her view of just the side of his face, she observed the similar shape of his eyes and the angle of his jaw.

Isobel noticed Susanna glancing between the man and Iain. "Susanna, this is Gawain. Gawain," —Isobel elbowed the man in the back of his ribs— "this is our guest, Susanna."

He turned, the dark-brown braid at his temple spilling over his shoulder as his dark, greenish eyes cast an impatient glance at her. Definitely related to Iain, in both his eye color and the power he barely restrained. He tipped his head respectfully but returned to his discussion, his fist pounding the table as he defended his position in a debate she hadn't caught the beginning of.

Susanna watched and waited. Everyone across the table began eating before she lifted her hands from her lap. In a flash of movement, Robert confiscated her plate before her fingers touched the silver, and she glanced to her left, surprised to find he hadn't put one piece of food on his plate either.

"Doona wait for me, Robert," she said.

He gave her a heavy look, arching a brow and staring for a brief moment, before turning toward the feast and loading her plate. He gave her generous helpings of venison; pheasant; stewed turnips, beets, and parsnips; and a piece of apple tart the size of her fist. He laid her plate onto the table with a clang.

Savory and sweet scents wafted up, making her mouth water. She lifted her provided two-pronged fork, twirling it between her fingers as she stared at the pile of food. "Robert, you've clearly mistaken my size. How am I to eat all this?"

He paused, sliding a peacock leg beside stewed kale on his plate. "Like we all do, Susanna: one bite at a time." Roars of laughter ignited on their end of the table at his loud remark, and she burst out laughing along with them.

"I shall do my best," she replied, snorting despite trying her damnedest not to.

Isobel smirked, glancing at Robert. "It's a plan to help himself to more food without looking like a pig." Isobel winked at her.

"'Twas not a plan, but should the lass not finish her plate, I'd be most happy to assist," Robert replied, his tone sober.

Susanna began eating, carefully chewing and savoring each bite. Conversations erupted all around her on topics ranging from the newest sword the smithy had crafted to the amount of snowfall they'd received over the last two days. The talk eventually shifted to the mysterious tree Robert's men had brought back from the forest.

"Well, gather around and see for yourself what the tree is all about." Isobel pressed her palms onto the edge of the table, attempting to stand. Iain shot behind her and assisted his wife, who smiled up at him, taking his aid with grace.

Benches and stools were moved from the tables and brought closer to the hearth. Piled under the lush pine tree were small objects of all shapes, wrapped in linen and tied with bright jewel-colored ribbons. The packages were neatly stacked upon a crimson and dark-green cloth bearing tiny designs embroidered in gold thread that glittered in the firelight. Isobel pulled her husband by the hand to a wide armchair nearest the tree.

Susanna hesitated, hovering near the outside edge of everyone, uncertain where to go. Robert gave her a gentle push toward another large, carved-wood armchair. He dropped onto the seat, yanking her down with him.

"Robert!" She gasped in surprise as she toppled into his lap. The second her bottom hit his hard thighs, she struggled to get up, but he banded his arms around her, and no amount of effort allowed her freedom from the compromising position.

He winced. "Easy, lass. You'll rip open the stitches in my side."

Her mouth fell open, then she shut it. "Doona take liberties not offered."

"I dinna take, Susanna. I *gave* you a seat." Robert smirked at her, a glint of mischief glimmering in his eyes.

"Fine," she huffed. "Keep your hands still, and I shall accept your offer." Her voice softened as she thought of his injury. "Does it hurt much?"

He tipped his head, gazing at her for a long moment. "Aye, it hurts a great deal. But I'd suffer the pain of a thousand sword strikes to have you safely in my arms."

Her skin flushed over her entire body, the warmest weight pressing heavy within her chest. "Thank you, Robert. I hope you never have to endure another scratch for me again. But . . ."

"What is it, Susanna?"

She sucked a slow breath through pursed lips, trying to calm a dark, unbidden panic creeping in from the fringes of her mind. "We let Dougal escape, and my father will stop at nothin' to force me to his will. While I'm here, I endanger you. I'm a risk to everyone here."

Robert tightened his embrace until she could hardly breathe, then loosened his hold. "Doona worry about your father or Dougal. No matter how they've threatened you, within these walls, you're under the shelter of my clan. Above all, you're protected by me."

She shook her head, unable to fathom mere walls keeping a beast like her father out. Tales of his astounding victories whispered into her memories like they had through Clan MacEalan's great hall. "You doona know what he's capable of."

"'Tis no matter, Susanna, for I know what I'm capable of. Abandon your worry. Let me handle anythin' threatenin' to harm you. Agreed?"

Susanna reluctantly nodded, even though neither the action nor his words did anything to allay her fears.

An echoing high-noted ring interrupted their conversation. Isobel stood next to the tree with a delicate metal bell in one hand and an ornately carved, ivory-handled dagger in the other.

"Thank you everyone for joining in our festivities for tonight. Where I come from we celebrate the birth of Jesus Christ in church—with our religious celebrations—and through a tradition we call Christmas. Christmas is a time where gifts are given to the ones we love to bring smiles to their faces and warmth into their hearts. Those gifts are called presents and are hidden beneath wrapping paper, adorned with ribbons, and placed under a tree.

"Tonight, we decorate the first Brodie Christmas tree. Each of you may have wondered about the specific favor I asked of you—for a tiny treasure to be crafted. Tonight, you'll each open the gift you created and hang them on a branch. They're called ornaments."

Isobel took a thin golden ribbon, looped it through the top of the small bell, and hung it from a branch in the middle of the tree. The weight of the metal dropped the branch a few inches. Susanna stared at the bell, watching it shine from the light of the fire as it gently swayed before settling. Amazed by the beauty of an event she'd become lucky enough to take part in, she glanced around and found everyone else watching with the same rapt interest.

"Hamish, since you've enabled this tree to be erected in our great hall with the iron stand you created to my precise specifications, you shall place the next ornament on the tree."

A burly man with sandy-brown hair stepped forward from the crowd. Iain assisted Isobel by squatting down and retrieving a small wrapped item with a green bow she'd pointed out to him, and he handed the item to Hamish. With a furrow to his brow and a serious expression on his face, Hamish's large fingers pulled on the tiny strings, and the ribbon and linen fell open, cradled in the palm of his hand. A tiny silver dagger no more than two inches long, with a sparkling emerald embedded in the cross of the hilt, lay in the middle of the wrapping.

Isobel took the item from his hand, looped another golden ribbon beneath the hilt, and handed it back to the smithy.

"Where shall I place it, M'Lady?" he asked.

"It's your choice, Hamish. That's the fun of decorating: there are no rules," Isobel replied.

The man nodded and placed the ornament higher up, moving the loop back over the pine needles until the branch dipped only a couple inches from the weight.

Iain spoke as the dagger spun in a slow circle. "Well done, Hamish."

Hamish joined his smiling wife who looked nearly as pregnant as Isobel. He stepped behind her and enfolded the happy woman in his arms.

"It's your turn, Robert—for leading the expedition to

bring us this exceptional Christmas tree, the beauty of which is rivaled only by the other gift you brought to us tonight, Susanna. Please honor us by placing your ornament on the tree," Isobel said.

"Susanna, will you hang the ornament for me?" Robert asked.

She looked into dark eyes filled with warmth. Her shyness among his clan melted away with the gentle intensity in his gaze. "'Tis an honor, Robert. Thank you," she whispered.

She eased off his lap, careful not to disturb his injury, and walked over to Isobel and Iain. Isobel pointed, and Iain plucked up a round, flat present, its wrapping made of ivory silk, tied with a thin red ribbon. It reminded Susanna of the wider ribbon that had bound her hands the day before.

How oddly fitting.

Her heartbeat accelerating in mild excitement, Susanna pulled the loose end of the ribbon. The bow unraveled, the silk fabric beneath falling open in a wisp across her palm. She pulled back the corners to see what lay hidden within. It was a delicate, pale wooden shape with six points, its surface polished to a high sheen.

"'Tis a snowflake," Robert said.

Susanna turned around. "You made this?"

"Aye. I carve more than bows for huntin'."

Susanna pulled the silk and ribbon away, closing her left fist around the soft material as she held the ornament up. Isobel threaded a golden loop through an opening on the delightful treasure. With trembling fingers and tears filling her eyes, Susanna stood on her tiptoes and hung the wooden snowflake high on a branch. She wanted Robert to see his exquisite ornament at eye level when he later stood in front of the tree.

The lightweight ornament spun in one direction, twisting on its ribbon loop, then unwound, spinning the other direction. She laughed and clapped her hands, pleased at how perfect it looked dangling from its branch. She glanced over at Robert. However, his attention was directed not on his ornament, but squarely on her, the intensity of his gaze heating her body once again.

She took a deep breath to steady herself and walked back to his chair. "May I return to my seat, Robert?"

Robert smiled, and she suddenly realized what had struck her earlier that she hadn't been able to place. He'd shaved. A face that had once held the rugged appeal of a week's worth of stubble had become all the more attractive clean-shaven.

She shook her head, shocked at her uninhibited thought. *Really, Susanna? Thinkin' a man handsome now?*

Robert opened his arms wide, and she settled onto his lap, facing more forward to better see the festivities. She wriggled a bit, trying to get more comfortable in the position.

A low groan rumbled into her ear. "Susanna, please. If you keep shakin' your ass against me like that, I might die right here in this chair."

She gasped, afraid she'd hurt his injury again. "I'm sorry, Robert. I doona wish you more pain."

He sighed and gripped her hips with his hands, stilling her movements. "'Tis fine, Susanna. I'm willin' to suffer."

Susanna exhaled slowly, trying to ignore an uncomfortable firmness beneath her bottom while remaining as still as possible to spare Robert further distress. She felt a twitch under her, and a flash of ache speared between her thighs. Her breath caught right as another groan came from Robert.

Understanding dawned on her as the dull pain turned erotic, spreading into delicious warmth. Robert suffered in the same way she now did: from the tortured pleasure of their bodies joined intimately as they sat together.

She swallowed hard, uncertain what she should do. She swept her gaze across the other faces in the room, but they all paid attention to Brigid as she hung a bluish glass icicle ornament on the tree.

Since her wriggling had seemed to make it worse for him . . . and for her . . . she focused on calming her breathing and sitting perfectly still on his lap. The task of maintaining complete stillness took great effort, as the more she tried to remain immobile against Robert's heat behind her, that hard twitching beneath her, and his intoxicating scent drifting around her, the more she wanted to . . . *move*.

Gawain was the next to place his ornament on the tree. She watched in quiet reverence as a solemn hush spread into the room. Hung from a delicate silver chain was an ornate gold and silver pendant that looked familiar. She leaned to the side and confirmed what she'd thought. At his hip, Iain wore a brooch fastened to his plaid that matched the pendant's design.

When Gawain dangled the necklace from a perch on a high branch, the dazzling jewel spun. He captured the twirling pendant with trembling fingers and slowly released it. On a deep breath, the enormous warrior stood back, staring at the tree while everyone in the room watched silently.

Iain came up behind Gawain and clapped him on the shoulder. "She'll be with us always, brother."

Robert whispered into Susanna's ear, "'Twas their mother's."

With a single hard nod, Gawain turned away from Iain, breaking their brief brotherly connection. Susanna tried to watch where he went, but he disappeared behind the people standing on the outer edge. She slowly exhaled, sharing in his pain.

One by one everyone present took a turn hanging their unique ornament on the tree. With all the rustling of the tree's branches and needles, the fragrant scent of a pine forest filled the space around them. After the last ribbon-wrapped present from under the tree had been hung, Isobel took a length of wider gold ribbon and wove it in and out of the branches, above, below, and behind the ornaments.

"I still have your ribbon, you know," Robert whispered in Susanna's ear.

"My ribbon?" she asked.

"Aye, the one that bound you . . . to keep you from harmin' me. I doona think the measure was unwise at the time," he teased.

He shifted, reaching his arm behind him, and pulled the length of wide red ribbon from the pleats at his waist. He placed it in her palm, folding her fingers over it. "Keep it. I retrieved it from the snow when I set you free."

When he set her free . . .

Had he? When every instinct she possessed and all the carefully trained moments of her life had been toward escaping imprisonment, could a man—the very thing she'd identified as the enemy—have granted her freedom . . . rather than her taking it?

No.

Freedom was earned. The blessedness of her life being her own could never be granted; it was taken. Seized at all costs. Risked at all peril.

Brigid appeared from the kitchen and handed them each a metal tankard. Susanna carefully held the handle of the etched cup as delicious spiced aromas rose on tendrils of steam from the amber liquid's surface.

Isobel and Iain also passed out the beverage that, even after the decadent meal Susanna consumed, made her mouth water anew. She handed her tankard to Robert and stood as everyone in the room rose from their seated positions.

Robert edged close behind her. "I believe a toast is forthcomin'," he whispered.

His hot breath fanned across her ear, sending another course of shivers through her. The heat of his body pressed into her back challenged her already weakening focus. She swallowed hard, took a deep breath, and tried to block out his presence.

She failed. Nothing muted his power over her. She furrowed her brow and continued to make the attempt anyway.

"Does everyone have a drink?" Isobel asked, glancing around.

Iain nodded to her.

"Good. Tonight is one of countless nights in many years to come where we will celebrate hope, faith, and love at Christmastime. Iain and I shall be wrapping presents to give to one another, and to those who need a smile brought to their face. We encourage you to do the same.

"Tonight, we drink spiced apple cider. It's a beverage

similar to your apple wine, and one my people drank around the holidays."

"No eggnog?" Iain interjected, a wry smile on his face.

"Shhh," Isobel chided.

He growled low.

She smiled.

Susanna watched the exchange, wondering about the couple's story. They were so clearly in love with one another and seemed perfectly suited, despite their chafing and grumbling.

Isobel continued, raising her spiced cider. Everyone followed in kind.

"To Clan Brodie! May we fight hard, love harder, and cherish every heart among us as we embrace what matters most during a season of giving. To Clan Brodie's first Christmas!"

"To Clan Brodie's first Christmas!" everyone shouted, the sentiment echoing into the rafters.

Susanna took a sip of the hot liquid, enjoying the sweet spicy taste rolling over her tongue. As soon as she turned, Robert wrapped his arms around her, and she tilted her face up to find him smiling broadly as he gazed down at her.

"I dinna know people could be so happy," she confessed, her voice soft to her own ears.

"I had no idea happiness was possible for me, *before you*," Robert said.

"Aren't you a part of this clan? How could you not be happy?"

"Ahhh, tonight, Isobel and Iain have invited only a few of our clan to celebrate in our first Christmas. There are many single women that are not here tonight . . ." He sighed. "Some women can be quite vicious and relentless when pursuin' a man they want."

"Women pursue men? This is a strange clan indeed," she remarked, surprised to hear about the women she hadn't yet met.

Robert barked out a laugh. "Aye, lass. With regard to that matter, I whole-heartedly agree. And now, with you in my arms, I realize why none of them ever appealed to me."

"Why is that?" she asked.

His expression grew tender, causing her breath to catch. "No woman ever gained my interest, because none of them were you."

Overwhelmed, and needing more air due to the building heat between them, she turned away from his penetrating gaze but remained within the comfort of his arms as she stared at Isobel's Christmas tree. A few small candles now flickered from within tiny glass jars that hung on only the sturdiest branches. Pieces made of gold and many other shining surfaces twinkled with light. Each person here tonight had placed a piece of themselves upon that tree—a collection of brilliant unique gifts brought together into one beautiful whole.

Her mark hadn't been left there, but she'd only come upon their family by happenstance, not plan. She felt detached from it all, an outsider in their unfamiliar world.

"Happiness . . . 'tis not possible for me, Robert."

He touched a finger under her chin, lifting her face to meet his dark eyes. "Everythin' is possible. When we least expect it and have given up all hope of findin' what we want, suddenly it appears in the most unlikely of places."

The words he spoke were amazing, and he made her want to believe. Her heart pounded with the excitement of what his idea promised . . . mixed with great fear of it not being true. She'd never had what Isobel had spoken of. And yet, in Robert's arms, it seemed within her grasp.

A fragile feeling of hope flickered within her heart like a newborn flame. She only wished she knew how to protect that delicate flame from the fierce wind blowing.

Suddenly, an unmistakable wave of power rippled through her body. She and Robert both snapped their heads toward the source.

She gasped. The magnificent black-winged creature stood in the entrance of the great hall.

"Robert, do you see . . . that?" she whispered.

He bent his head down, whispering, "Aye, love. 'Tis quite the sight."

"'Twas not my imagination," she said.

"Nay. His name is Skorpius. And he ... *aids* ... Lady Isobel from time to time," Robert said.

"But he ... he has ..."

"Aye. Wings. 'Tis a real-life angel." Robert hesitated, his voice dropping lower, "Brodie Castle possesses a great amount of magick that I need to properly explain when we have the time."

Susanna couldn't take her eyes off the breathtaking creature. A wild mane of black hair framed a beautiful face with eyes like faceted jewels that glittered between emerald and sapphire. Wings of darkest midnight arched high above his shoulders, their long-feathered tips nearly brushing the gray stone floor. His chest and arms were muscular and bare—his only attire: black leather pants and worn, black leather boots with their strings untied.

Isobel made her way toward Skorpius, waddling between the chairs and tables with Iain right by her side.

"Warrior-of-time turned holiday-errand-boy, at your service," Skorpius announced.

"Oh, pipe down, Cupcake. You grumble more than an old woman crippled with arthritis," Isobel said.

A growl reverberated so deeply from the creature, Susanna's bones vibrated.

A green bundle hung from a red ribbon in Skorpius' fist.

"What's danglin' from the ribbon in his hand?" Susanna asked a bit too loudly.

"It's mistletoe," Isobel replied.

Skorpius muttered, "*Enchanted* mistletoe, as none grows here. I stole this from a Victorian entryway in the dark of night, circa 1867."

"Shush, Cupcake. I'm warning you." Isobel glared at him. "Hang it from the hook above you."

The warrior stood easily a foot taller than any Brodie clansman and with a single reach up, he caught the ribbon on a hook embedded into a thick wooden crossbeam over his head. "Keep calling me Cupcake and nothing will shush me," he grumbled.

"What is *he* doin' here?" Brigid shouted.

Skorpius fell silent at the sound of Brigid's voice. His

chest rose and fell more deeply as he stared at her, and the feeling of animosity from the creature vanished, affection emanating from him instead.

Susanna blinked hard at the change . . . *that she felt.*

"What is this *mistletoe* for?" Robert asked.

"It's from an ancient Norse legend. Those that stand under the mistletoe are to kiss. It brings the couple luck and good health. It's a symbol of peace, of love. I've always made a wish during the kiss," Isobel replied.

Robert suddenly grabbed Susanna's hand and pulled her through the crowd. She tugged her hand back, trying to resist him, but in spite of her attempts to escape his iron grip, he dragged her toward the front door.

"Let me go, you brute!" Susanna growled.

Conversations fell silent as Susanna dug her heels into the wooden floor, the scrapes sounding shrill to her ears; she imagined shavings flying up in her wake. Despite her resistance, Robert's unyielding hold and his supreme strength powered their momentum until he stopped and turned to face her, directly under the hung mistletoe.

He'd halted so abruptly, Susanna crashed into his chest. Before she could push away, his arms folded around her, banding hers to her sides.

He crushed an unexpected kiss onto her lips. She gasped and his tongue gained entrance, his sizzling heat and demanding possession overpowering her. On a sigh, she melted into his arms, taking everything Robert gave as delicious warmth spread through her body.

A sensation rippled through her, and a distant memory of a wish echoed and floated away. . . . *that God would have love embrace them . . .*

"Seeee . . ." Isobel grinned at the kissing couple while elbowing Skorpius. "Look what you did."

Skorpius grunted.

"I've decided I *will* stop calling you Cupcake," she

declared. "Now, I'm calling you Cupid."

His booming voice shifting into her head made her jump. *"Don't even* think *about it, Runt."*

She laughed. "Oh, yes. Cupid. Delicious, sweet, pink-icing covered Cupcake has now been renamed Cupid."

He growled to her right.

It was interrupted by Brigid's scathing quip to her left. "That angel wouldn't know love if it dropped as a two-thousand-pound boulder on his head."

Isobel always *felt* Skorpius's presence when he appeared within the castle, but she wondered if Brigid sensed his immutable power as her sister-in-law turned on her heel and crossed to the far side of the room, distancing herself as much as physically possible from the angel. Brigid fired a scorching glare toward Skorpius that would easily flay the skin off a mere mortal.

Isobel arched an eyebrow at him in question.

His reply was a non-negotiable, imperceptible shake of his head.

Chapter Nine

Robert pulled away from Susanna once she'd given herself over to the moment completely. In his arms, under the assault of his kiss, she'd surrendered herself. No more fighting. No more doubts. When she abandoned all the troubling thoughts in her head and lost herself to passion, she became someone more than the woman who'd nearly trampled him in a snowfield trying to escape. She transformed into a woman living for something greater than her miserable past.

Any supposed treaty-bound right Dougal may have had to Susanna ceased to exist the moment she'd escaped her fate. With fierce determination, she'd run from that wretched life and landed straight within Robert's shielding arms. He vowed to *bury* her past. From the depths of his once-jaded heart, he intended to be her present and future.

Dark blue eyes gazed up at him, her black pupils blown wide. He smiled. With a tight hold around her, since all of her slight weight had fallen against him, he pushed his arms outward, leaning her upright. "You're glorious when you put up a fight, Susanna," he whispered

She swallowed, dropping her gaze to his lips. "I doona know about that, Robert, but ... your kisses ... rob me of the verra air I need to breathe."

He smiled, tapping the tip of her nose with his finger. "I assure you, there'll be plenty of breathin' when we kiss. I doona want you passin' out."

Over her shoulder, he caught Iain staring at them with unveiled irritation. A discussion with his laird was long overdue. Not wanting to leave Susanna alone, he ushered her over to Isobel and Brigid, companions she seemed to like and that he could safely leave her with.

Susanna spoke up the moment they joined the two women. "Isobel, how did you and Iain meet?"

Isobel laughed and exchanged a glance with Brigid, who lifted her eyebrows. "It's a very long and unbelievable story, one to be saved for when we have hours of time just the two of us."

Brigid offered, "The crux of the matter is the Universe conspired against them . . . or *for* them . . . to make both of their stubborn minds see what was important."

Isobel laughed. "Well said, sister."

Robert interjected, "Ladies, please excuse me. I must talk with Iain." He lifted his hand from the small of Susanna's back, but curled his fingers over his empty palm once he severed their connection, immediately missing direct contact with her.

Iain waited at the entrance of the dark hallway that led beyond the kitchen and larder toward his map room. The grim look on Iain's face, and the other glares he'd sent through the course of the night, foretold that their encounter promised to be an unpleasant one. Robert faced his laird in a relaxed wide stance with his back to the great hall.

"What were you thinkin'?" Iain asked.

"She needed refuge," he replied.

Iain crossed his arms over his chest, dropping his chin down, glaring at him from beneath his thick brows. "You're not offerin' the lass temporary refuge. You've claimed her."

"Aye, I have," Robert replied.

"Is she prepared for what that entails?" Iain asked.

Robert snorted. "She's not yet realized that I've claimed her. The rest will come in time."

"We doona have the luxury of time in our world. You know that, Robert. I've a clan to protect, and you've put them at great risk by bringin' her here."

"I'll settle the matter with her soon," Robert offered.

"Tonight. You'll explain to a woman, whom Isobel tells me escaped from her castle and everythin' she's known, that she's now a prisoner here. She needs to know she canna ever leave. You've sealed that fate for her. *Tonight*."

A sound alerted them both, and Robert turned. Susanna stood a few feet away at the foot of the stairs with her hand over her mouth, her eyes widening. She turned and ran.

"Or now . . ." Iain's words drifted off as Robert tore after her.

"Susanna!"

Robert saw the deep scowl on her face, but Susanna fled, lifting her skirt into her clenched fists as she charged up the stairs. He jumped onto the third one from the side, taking the stone steps two at a time to catch her.

By the time he hit the landing, she'd already sprinted down the entire hall and burst through her bedchamber door. Robert gave his legs everything they had and slid inside after her, crashing into the frame and the edge of the oak door right as she slammed it shut. The door sprung back and hit Susanna, throwing her backward onto the fur rug on the floor before it banged shut behind him.

"Susanna!" He rushed to pull her up to make certain she wasn't injured.

She yanked her hand away from his outstretched one, remaining where she sat, the silk of her deep-ruby gown heaped around her. "Nay. I'll not be kept prisoner here."

He lowered down onto his knees before her. "'Tis not like you imagine, Susanna."

"Oh? I'd be free to come and go as I pleased?" she asked.

"Without question," he said.

She narrowed her eyes at him. "Even if I chose to leave forever?"

He sighed. "Weel, not exactly. I hope in time, you'll never want to leave."

The delicate woman came alive at the suggestion, leaning forward on her knees like a deadly snake ready to strike. "Those were the kind of words spoken to Mama. When Broc *stole* her away. He threatened her. *Hurt her*. Things she endured for the love of her family—for the love of me."

She pressed further forward, and Robert leaned back onto his heels for fear she'd actually bite.

"Doona promise me the *last* thing I would want in this world."

Her nostrils flared and her chest heaved. His heart went out to her. She'd clearly lived a horrific life, and he only understood the tiny fragments she'd just shared in her fury.

He sighed and pressed forward before she toppled onto him. She backed off by inches until they both knelt upright, almost touching, staring deep into each other's eyes. He brushed a stray curl away from her flushed cheek and buried his fingers into her soft hair, gazing down at her.

Hurt, fear, and hope all reflected back to him from eyes that grew glassy with tears. He inhaled slowly, calming the warrior within him longing to do battle for every wrong committed against the innocent, but very brave, woman before him. Instead, he focused on being the gentle man who desperately needed to soothe away the pain she held deep inside. "Susanna, know this, and listen to me carefully: no one will ever hurt you. I will do everythin' within my power to protect you, even if it means dyin' for you. You'll stay here at Brodie Castle as long as you seek my protection. I'd only hoped you'd never want to leave—" he swallowed hard "—because you seek my love."

Those shimmering blue eyes blinked. She stared at him before lifting her trembling hands to his face. He closed his eyes, reveling in the warm touch of her fingertips across his jaw and up to his cheeks.

"Is that what you're offerin', Robert?" she asked, her voice but a whisper.

He opened his eyes, pinning her with a hard look. "I'll offer you the world. If you want the sun and moon snatched down from the sky, I'll hunt them down and bring them to you. The countless stars that glitter in the night shall become jewels adornin' your hair. All the oceans wide will be yours to traverse, and each creature shall treat you as friend and master.

"As for me—" he dropped his lips to her forehead,

grazing them across her soft skin "—my heart belongs to you, my soul is yours, and my body yearns to give you pleasure like you've never imagined."

Susanna's breath caught, and she lowered her face as a lovely blush spread across her high cheekbones. He tucked a finger under her chin, holding her gaze captive, if nothing else. The brave lass in his arms took a deep breath and straightened taller, pressing closer into his body. As she stared back at him, an inner strength manifested in her eyes, and she dropped her hands onto his waist and slid them behind him, just below his bandaged injury.

"I do want what you offer, Robert. But I . . . I'm afraid."

"Do you trust that I won't hurt you?" he asked, not moving a muscle for fear of startling the fragile creature who'd willingly embraced him.

"Aye. I do trust you," she replied, those sapphire eyes holding *him* captive.

"Then doona be afraid. Fear and worry are your past now. All you'll ever have will be safety and happiness. It shall become my life's mission."

Her lush lower lip trembled, and he was lost. He dropped his head, and captured those tempting lips, savoring her sweet taste, teasing her with slow sucks. He eased his head back to brush his lips across hers, before pressing back in, licking his tongue across the seam and sliding in deeper as she sighed.

Susanna gripped his lower back with her hands, pulling his hips toward hers as their kiss intensified, her tongue flicking into his mouth and tangling with his. A low moan came from her throat, and he groaned, wanting to take his time despite the urgent desire in his loins.

His hands drifted down from her hair, behind her ears, and skimmed down her graceful neck. He placed small kisses along her jaw and beneath it, his lips following the rapid pulse beneath her skin to her delicate collarbone. With deft fingers, he pulled apart the laces holding her gown in place and the material shifted, sliding down her shoulders.

Susanna inhaled deeply and pulled back, looking up at him as his hands slid her gown and chemise past her hips into a pool of material at her knees. She shivered, the cool air in the room teasing across her exposed skin, her breasts tightening, pink nipples hardening.

He stared at her in awe. The fire from the hearth danced shadows and light across her porcelain skin, over curves gifted generously by God. His gaze drifted up from her perfect form into trusting eyes. "Damn, Susanna. If you kill me tonight, I shall die the happiest man on Earth."

A small smile graced her face, and she inhaled a shaky breath. "There shall be no dyin'. Not tonight."

She fisted her hands beside her, opened and lifted them, but hesitated then let them fall by her sides again. Something held her back from taking what she wanted. He furrowed his brow, concerned that fear still stood in her way. He hoped her timidity stemmed from inexperience. No matter the reason, he intended to banish everything holding her back tonight.

As she knelt before him, bared and unafraid, his heart warmed. He wanted to touch her again, but he desperately needed skin on skin. He had an urgent need to heat her with a slow molten flame, igniting deep to burn forever.

He pulled her slippers from her feet and eased her down onto the fur rug, supporting her shoulders with his hand as he swept the remaining fabric away from her exquisite body. She lay on her back, naked, one knee bent, looking up at him with wonder in her eyes, her chest rising and falling.

"Lass, in all my life, I've never seen, nor will I ever see, such a breathtakin' sight."

Holding her gaze, he unfastened and discarded his boots. He released the pin holding his tartan, and the material fell loose before he tossed it aside. For a brief moment, he broke eye contact, yanking the linen shirt over his head—and he never wanted to lose sight of her again.

Her smile widened. "Robert, you're a remarkable sight to behold yourself." Her brow furrowed slightly as her gaze fell onto the thin strip of linen bandaged around his lower ribs.

"I assure you, 'tis but a scratch." Emboldened by her appreciation and worry, he lowered himself down beside her. Her surrender was a precious gift, one he intended to savor and cherish.

He feathered the backs of his fingertips over her skin starting at the base of her throat and tracing down to her navel. She responded to his teasing, closing her eyes and instinctively arching upward toward his slight touch.

He turned his hand over and stroked back up across her soft skin, skimming his fingers over her quivering belly, up the center of her chest, and along the side of her neck. "Look at me, Susanna."

Her eyes fluttered open, darkened with lust. She lifted a hand and cupped his cheek. Elated, he leaned into the tender caress, turning his face and kissing her palm. To be touched and desired by a woman who wanted him for the man within, and no other reason, stuttered his heart. He dipped his head, capturing her lips, needing more of everything she generously offered. She kissed him back with renewed force, setting fire to his veins.

He broke their kiss with a nip of her lips, and a low whimper came from her throat. She shifted her legs and stretched them straight, squirming as she swayed her hips, rubbing her thighs together.

She sought relief.

Woman, you'll go up in flames first.

A glance at her face revealed she'd closed her eyes again. Her lips had parted slightly.

He smirked and lowered his mouth to her nipple, licking the hardened tip. A loud gasp came as she opened her mouth wide. Her breast lifted, and her fingers speared into his hair as he sucked the tip past his tightened lips. She moaned low, exhaling, but he held on, keeping his newfound treasure locked tight between his teeth as he suckled.

She thrashed her head to the right, whimpering under his intimate assault. When he thought she could bear no more, he released her nipple and watched it spring back, glistening and red. He blew gently on it as his gaze met her widened eyes.

"Robert . . . I . . ." Her chest heaved as she fell silent in her bewilderment.

"Aye, lass. You do. Spectacularly."

He leaned over her, seizing her other nipple, and drifted his hand down. He skimmed an open palm across her belly until his fingers sifted through soft, black curls. With care, he grazed his fingers over her mound, teasing over her lips, and then he slid his hand between her upper thighs, pressing them open. She obeyed his unspoken command, spreading her legs further apart.

"That's a good lass," he whispered against her breast.

She trembled as he slid his fingers back up through her folds, her slick moisture coating them. He pulled his head up, watching her face as he touched the flesh around her nerve center. With a firm grasp, he pinched the soft hood at the base between two fingers and gently pulled up.

A loud cry ripped from her throat and her hips arched off the rug against his hand. He smiled down at her as he released the hold on her most sensitive spot, lowering his fingers down, massaging in slow circles. She groaned, closing her eyes again as she tossed her head back into the rug.

He dropped his head to her exposed neck, sucking small, wet kisses in a line up to her ear. With increased pressure from his fingers, he had her writhing beneath his touch, small moans coming from her throat with every breath.

"Give in to the pleasure, lass. Let it take you over," he whispered. He softly sucked her earlobe, licking it with the tip of his tongue while she shivered.

As her moans grew deeper and louder, he slid his fingers lower, pressing one into her tight entrance. He continued circling her nerve center with his thumb as he eased a second finger into her, pressing further.

A tiny whimper came from Susanna's throat, and he paused as her taut entrance clamped around his fingers. Instant understanding penetrated his sensually fogged brain. Relief that she'd never been touched rivaled a great sense of pride in his realization: he was the honored one to have her. Stretching her with care, he found the spot inside that rippled from her arousal. He circled his fingertips over the sensitive area in rhythm to his thumb rubbing her clit.

Susanna went wild, her cries echoing against the stone walls of her bedchamber. He captured her mouth, silencing her while she brilliantly came apart at his hand. With their consuming kiss, he swallowed her guttural scream as hard spasms gripped his fingers and racked her body with tremors.

She kissed him with uninhibited passion, her tongue tangling and fighting with his, her moans softening. He slowed the pace of his massage, soothing her tissues with his touch.

Pride welled stronger in his chest; he'd caused her that pleasure. The feisty woman who'd once threatened his life had utterly surrendered to his touch.

He pulled away from her, needing to hear it from her lips. "Susanna?"

Her eyes fluttered open, glassy with moisture, darkened with desire. "Aye, Robert."

He stayed his hand, staring deep into her eyes. "You must offer yourself to me freely, completely; because, the moment I take you, you're mine. You'll belong to me . . . with no chance for escape."

A wide smile spread across her face. "I never want to leave your arms, Robert. Take me . . . I'm yours."

Susanna's powerful words were sweeter than he'd imagined. "Aye, lass. You are mine."

With a fierce need to be one with her, he tightened his grip over her mound and within her, stealing her gasp with a deep kiss. He shifted his weight, moving between her legs. In utter reverence, he kissed a trail along the skin of her neck and down between her breasts, sipping, tasting, gently nipping as he crouched lower, forcing her to spread her silky thighs wider.

The scent of her arousal drifted around them, sweet and musky, calling to him. He glanced up and held her gaze as he dipped his mouth and flattened his tongue against her in a long firm swipe. The honeyed taste of her essence drew a low growl from his throat, something primal deep within him awakening. Undone, he dropped his mouth over her clit and sucked hard.

Her rasping moan shot straight to his throbbing shaft. He had to have her, could wait no longer.

He steadied his breathing and climbed her splendid body that she'd spread wide open, all for him. She gazed at him in sensual-drugged wonder while he held his face inches above hers. He stilled his body, holding on to the treasured moment as long as possible, but she arched into him, her lips colliding with his.

On a growl, he pressed her back into the rug, his shaft aligned straight up through her slickened folds. He kissed her with all the passion he felt in his heart for the hellion who had tamed him, had dared to make him want more— offered him the entire world on such a blessed night.

With a shaky breath, he broke their kiss as he eased his hips back. Dreamy eyes stared up at him.

"This'll hurt a wee bit," he said, furrowing his brow as he pressed his hand up the back of her thigh, gently urging her bent knee up and out to the side.

A tiny smile tugged at the corners of her kiss-swollen lips. "You promised never to hurt me."

He leaned forward, his throbbing cock sliding through her juices, over her lit nerves. She gasped, arching her entire body against his. He kissed her, long and slow. "Only this once, Susanna. Then never again."

She relaxed back, her lips parting on a shaky sigh. "Do what you must, Robert. I ache inside for you. My world will not be complete 'til you're inside me . . . in every way."

A searing heat bloomed in his chest at her words. "Aye, love."

He pulled his hips back, watching her shudders, hearing her gasps—feeling need and want so deeply moving, he grew certain he'd never again be the same man. In the room's orange glow of firelight, they held each other's awestruck gaze, hearts racing, shallow breaths matching.

His cock caught at her entrance, and he pressed in to the slightest degree, pausing. She squirmed, her hips shifting. The overwhelming sensation rocking through him, shooting straight from their connection, took his breath away.

In a desperate bid to restrain himself, he circled his hips, feeling her tight muscles grip the tip of his shaft. The delightful creature wanting him—who had asked for him to take her—moaned in pleasure. He panted, furrowing his brow as her eyes drifted shut.

"Look at me, Susanna. I want to see your eyes as I claim you. When I embed myself deep inside you, you will know who owns you."

Susanna's eyes widened as he thrust forward. A soft cry escaped her lips. He fell forward, caging his body around her, straining to hold still as her tight, untried body gripped him. A whimper came from her lips as she pressed them to his temple. He dropped his head, kissing the shell of her ear before drifting lower and brushing his mouth beneath the lobe, sucking the tender skin between his lips. Each heated touch, every breathy sound, and her sweet taste seared him from the inside out.

"Easy, love. I'm goin' to move, now. Tell me if I hurt you," he whispered.

He eased back, withdrawing almost entirely as her inner muscles clutched his shaft. With concentration, he pressed forward, and she groaned. He opened his eyes, unaware he'd pinched them shut, and watched her. An innocent face that God himself had surely designed for this angel stared up at him in wonder as he slid back into her depths.

On another drawback, he swiveled his hips, eliciting a moan from her so low, the sound resembled the purr of a cat. With her eyelids half-fallen in drowsy sensual pleasure, she gave him a tender smile.

"Does it please you, Susanna?"

"Aye, Robert. It pleases me greatly," she said, sliding the palms of her hands along his sides, over his hips, and onto his buttocks. She dug her fingers into his skin, pulling his hips toward her as he thrust into her again.

Susanna threw her head back, crying out when he thrust hard at her urging. She lifted her other leg, pressing her heels into his ass. He pulled back faster and drove in deep. She arched her hips up and met his thrust. The timid lass he'd laid upon the rug only moments ago had vanished, a lustful woman taking her place.

She placed her lips at the base of his throat, drawing on his flesh with a hard suck. A low moan vibrated against his skin as she released her mouth and latched higher onto the side of his neck. Her fingernails pricked his hips, pulling and releasing in time with his movements.

He groaned as pleasure raced through him, shooting a demanding ache deep into his loins. As her exhalations came on low moans, each growing louder than the one before, perspiration dampened his brow from the enormous effort it took to hold back. He focused on his forced-slow breaths, waiting for her impending release to come first.

The pressure increased with her slightest movements, and he used his final, unraveling threads of strength to withstand the fiery heat surrounding his cock as her sounds turned to untamed cries. On a last torturous plunge, he held firm, rock hard and straining, as she careened toward the edge. He felt it, her hard spasm clamping around his shaft, as she gasped for air.

In that split second, sparks fired before his eyes, his entire body tightened, and he thrust deeper with a primal growl. Her scream echoed off the stone walls before he captured her lips in his, muffling their sounds. Her hands shot behind his head and pulled his hair at the scalp as she kissed him with renewed fervor, her hips grinding against him as he settled against her, deep within her. While his pulses ended, her tight spasms continued around him, one after the other, and she sobbed into their kiss.

A long sigh escaped his lungs as he stroked her tongue gently with his, her body relaxing beneath him. Their chests rose and fell hard, connecting their pounding hearts together with each gasping breath.

He broke their kiss and dropped his head, lightly touching her dampened forehead. With great tenderness, he stroked her cheek with his right thumb.

She leaned into the touch. "Robert?"

"Aye, my love," he whispered, kissing her temple.

"Is it always like that?" she asked.

"Nay, no encounter has ever come close," he replied.

"Why?"

His deep chuckle rumbled out. "Weel, for many reasons. I've never taken a maiden, I've never felt such deep emotion for any woman I've been with . . . and I've never been with a woman I intended to keep."

The shift of her entire body drew his face away from her neck, and he looked into her eyes. Her brows furrowed as she stared up at him.

"You said that earlier . . . that you *own* me." Her scowl deepened.

The hellion had returned. He smiled. "Aye. I do. I've owned you from the moment I laid eyes on you. Before you knew it—before I even knew it—you were mine," he said.

Susanna gaped at him. He forced himself not to laugh, understanding that everything she'd recently gone through was a considerable adjustment for someone who'd been so sheltered—and emotionally abused.

She squirmed, unintentionally tightening her inner muscles around his still slightly engorged cock. He groaned.

"I'll not be owned by anyone," she growled. "Get off me."

He did as she asked, slipping slowly from her. She let out a soft moan as they parted, but he groaned loudly as her slick body slid across his charged nerves. While their unrestrained sounds faded, she scowled anew—as if it were his fault she'd felt more pleasure—and flipped over on the rug.

"Oh, hell," he grumbled.

"What?" she huffed, turning her face to the side, causing the waves of her dark hair to slide across her porcelain skin.

Unable to stop himself, he rolled over her, covering her body once again. "If you thought to punish me by showin' me your flawless backside, you were gravely mistaken."

She bucked back, resisting his hold, but he pinned her hips down onto the bearskin rug, immobilizing her. He brushed his lips alongside an exposed portion of her neck, exhaling across her skin. She shuddered, her body clearly affected by his touch, regardless of what her rebellious mind wanted.

"How much do you know about weddin' and handfastin'?" he asked.

"What? I . . . I doona know anythin' other than a weddin' is a ceremony to bind a husband and wife."

"Aye," he replied, dragging his lips higher to rest right

beneath her ear as he shifted his hips, his shaft aligning with the cleft of her pert little ass. "When a maiden and a man unite physically, one for the other with heart and body, they're handfasted in the eyes of the church. Our clan recognizes those sacred laws."

"What . . . what are you sayin'?" she shook her head, arching her neck away from his lips.

He moved a hand up to her head, letting his hips continue to pin her body, and brushed her hair over her left shoulder, gripping it tight within his fist. He dropped his lips back to her ear, sucking the lobe into his mouth. "Aye, you belong to me. But I also belong to you. We're now husband and wife."

He wanted to elaborate on his feelings; he'd become more a prisoner to her than she'd be in any way. He needed to clarify Iain's concerned words; Brodie Castle held secrets and magick entrusted to the protection of their clan, a clan which now included her and relied upon her confidence. But with her delectable body and feisty spirit battling not against him, but her own desires, far greater wants and needs coursed hot through his veins, clouding sound logic.

Susanna growled deep in frustration, struggling beneath him with renewed strength. No amount of force she exerted, however, allowed her to move with the way he'd pinned her head and hips—leverage had its advantages.

"Submit to me, Susanna. Admit what I know you feel for me. Give yourself over, and I promise you unendin' pleasure and happiness," he said.

With his free hand, he brushed the side of her hip, trailed light fingertips along the dip at her waist, and caressed the side of her breast. He continued further, sliding his hand in beneath her, until he captured an already hardened nipple between his finger and thumb.

Her breath accelerated, but she remained rigid and perfectly still. He rolled her nipple and pinched it, lightly at first, then with increasing pressure. A moan came from her throat followed by a long growl, as if she'd grown angry at her own body.

"Well, Susanna? 'Tis your choice. I'll not take what's not

freely given," he said.

She held her breath, her every movement stilling. He stayed his hand, holding her entire body firmly as he waited.

"Aye, Robert," she whispered.

"Aye, Robert . . . what?" he asked, tightening his hold at the hair at her nape, drawing her head back as he pinched her nipple harder.

"I . . . submit."

Chapter Ten

Whatever power Robert possessed, it had more effect on Susanna than any amount of ale or spiced cider, casting her harrowing fears into faded memories. She had fallen under his spell and somehow couldn't imagine being anywhere else. His incredible heat and power surrounded her, and all she wanted, what her body and heart, her very *soul* craved, was to be desired by him, to be protected by him . . . *to be his*.

"Doona move," he warned, his voice rasping out, vibrating the skin of her throat.

A soft laugh escaped her lips. "I canna move."

As he held her head back with her hair fisted in his hand, his devastating lips dragged down the side of her neck and across her shoulder, burning her skin with slow kisses along the way. An unquenchable fire built within her again, the ravenous need of her body overcoming lucid thought.

She swallowed hard. He seemed perfectly content to spend an eternity with his mouth on her shoulder blade. Unable to stand the increasing need within her, she squirmed beneath his hips, trying to ease the tension. For a moment, pleasure coursed through her, the friction against the rug creating a new, exciting sensation.

A loud growl at her ear and hard tug of her head back made her freeze. She whimpered, her scalp stinging, while a surprising erotic heat radiated down, stoking her building fire.

"I said, 'doona move,' and I meant it," he clipped out.

"Robert, I canna help it. I *need* to move," she replied.

"Aye, love," he crooned, his heated breath trekking over the shell of her ear, "I know you do. Be patient. The reward is greater, the longer we wait."

A heavy sigh whooshed out of her lungs, her feisty nature holding true no matter his wishes. His low chuckle followed.

Silken strands of his hair brushed across her shoulders as he placed his teeth on the skin between her shoulder and neck. He bit down into the muscle; but instead of hurting, an aching pulse shot straight between her thighs. She gasped in shock. He released the primal hold, licking the skin and blowing on it. Goose bumps raced down her body.

"Do you trust me, lass?"

Did she? No one had held her trust other than Mama. She never thought another soul could hold it. Not in her wildest imaginings would she have thought *a man* could . . . or would. Yet Robert had proved he was no ordinary man. The impossible had become possible with him.

"Aye, Robert. Unbelievable as it seems to me, I trust you."

He shifted above her, dropping his thighs between her legs. With his one hand still fisted around her hair, he pressed the other into the rug beside her. His knees put pressure between her legs, and he leaned forward, pulling her with him. She found herself on her knees with her hips in the air, her legs spread wide on the outside of his thighs, and her upper body pressed into the rug. She felt exposed. Vulnerable.

A firm pressure pushed at her entrance. Another pulse of pleasure fired into her from their point of contact. She steadied her breathing, preparing herself. No matter the pleasure that he'd brought her, the last time he'd entered her, it felt as if he'd pierced and stretched her just under the point of breaking.

However, Robert didn't press in. While only the tip of his cock was lodged inside her entrance, he circled his hips. Without warning, he pulled out completely, and she groaned until he glided forward, his shaft sliding along her outside folds until he hit the spot that took her breath away. She gasped. He pressed forward, then eased back, forward and back, gliding across nerve endings that sparked alive at his touch.

Pressure within her grew, a devastating ache growing, and still she couldn't do anything to satisfy her need. She desperately wanted to move—tried to—but Robert's arm lay across her left shoulder blade, still gripping her hair, and her legs were locked into position, his knees between them.

Finally, she managed to rock her hips back.

Robert froze on a growl. "Nay."

As if sensing her frenzy, he pulled back and lodged his tip into her again. Against her bottom, he circled his hips, his shaft moving at her entrance, teasing her, taunting her. She panted, desperate for more.

Robert shifted again, the heat of his palm sliding over her right hip. It moved forward, across her lower belly, into her curls. She cried out the moment he touched her, a jolt of fiery pleasure clenching her muscles around his tip.

He groaned, sliding in only a fraction, before pulling back out, teasing her once again. With slow strokes of his fingers, he rubbed between her legs. Her panted breaths turned into moaned whimpers as raging desire threatened to overcome her. She moved back, and he froze, halting everything that felt good.

She gritted her teeth and focused on her breathing, wanting to please him, *needing* to obey him so he would please her. His fingers resumed their decadent torture, fueling the aching fire through her center once again.

"Good. Lass." His growled words seemed to come from far away, muted by the racing blood thundering in her ears.

On the edge.

Robert kept her on the brink of explosive pleasure. Each time she'd get close, he'd slow his movements, calming the raging fire down to a low-roaring hum. She caught her breath and moaned deep, letting all the air out of her lungs. His pace increased for a countless time, and the pleasurable pain grew to near-unbearable. She dangled on the precipice of falling over, but tried to quiet her cries, hoping he wouldn't know she was close . . . so he wouldn't withdraw the intensity again.

Somehow he knew, because his fingers slowed again, and she hung there. Her body tightened into a savage bundle of craving need. She couldn't take it anymore, couldn't handle the pressure . . . needed the pleasure.

"Robert . . . *please* . . ." she begged.

"Please . . . *what?*" he asked.

Did he chuckle?

"Please take me, Robert! I need you inside of me!" she cried.

His hand went wild against her, and she sobbed, desperate and at his mercy.

"Aye, you do, lass. You need me *deep* inside of you. I'll bury myself down so far, to remove me would tear out a piece of your soul."

She panted, his words searing her heart, his touch setting her body ablaze. Her breath caught as a hard pulse fired within her. Robert plunged deep, spearing her. Hard hot spasms followed, and she screamed, burying her face into the rug.

Robert released her hair and braced his forearms tight against her sides as he rocked hard into her body, each thrust firing off more staggering pulses. She fisted both hands into the soft fur and turned her face to the side, trying to suck air into her lungs as wave after wave of pleasure flowed through her body.

She couldn't move if she wanted to . . . and she didn't. Robert gripped her hips and pulled himself almost out. The shift caused him to penetrate her at a different angle. His quick, shallow strokes caused a new pleasure, and it fired through her like a bright bolt of lightning.

"Robert!" she screamed his name as another round of spasms claimed her, shuddering her entire body.

He gripped her hips harder, thrusting deeper, each delicious wave crashing one after another inside of her, around him. Her throat had gone dry from panting and moaning, and yet, she couldn't quiet her cries.

A feral growl ripped from Robert's chest into the room, drowning out her mewling sounds as his entire body stiffened. She felt a hot rush inside her body, distinctive pulses from his release mixing with hers.

His movements quieted, and she sighed. He lowered down to her side, scooping her backward into his warm embrace. A great peace filled her heart as her magnificent warrior wrapped himself around her, holding her tight while remaining embedded inside of her.

Her warrior.

He'd been right. He was already deep within her . . . already a part of her soul.

"Robert?" she whispered.

She felt his racing heart against her back. His deep breaths helped calm her breathing too, and she felt the beat of her heart begin to slow, matching his.

Warm. Protected. Cherished. She'd never thought it possible, but in a man's arms, she'd found the one thing she'd wanted most in her dark world . . . love.

"Robert?" she said louder.

"Mmm?"

"Will it always be like this?" she asked, her voice sounding dreamy to her own ears.

Tender lips placed a soft kiss to her shoulder blade. "Nay, love. 'Twill be better."

She wrapped her hands around the muscular forearm nestled between her breasts. "Impossible. How could it be better than that? I'll surely die if 'tis any more intense."

A low rumble vibrated against her back as his chest shook. The unexpected laughter amid something so serious made her smile.

"Lass, I've gone easy on you tonight. I'll tease and worship your body 'til you shake with need, then I'll give you the pleasure you crave, over and over . . . and over again."

She sighed at the enticing thought, still not understanding how it could be true. But she did what he'd asked and what she had honestly admitted to; she trusted him. Her eyes grew heavy as Robert's breathing fell steady, and she drifted away peacefully in his arms.

A sudden draft of cool air ran across Susanna's back, and she shivered. Disoriented, she pushed herself up off the rug and looked around to find she was alone in the bedchamber.

Uncertain where Robert had gone, but exhausted from everything he'd demanded from her body, she eased back onto the floor and stretched. He must've stoked the fire in the hearth, because a strong heat emanated from it, and its glow illuminated more of the cozy room she'd been given.

She looked up at the large space from her low vantage point. The perfectly made bed had intricately carved bedposts. Two armchairs and a table sat beside the hearth. Next to the bed, a small stand held the ceramic pitcher that Brigid had used earlier to wash Susanna's hair, and a shallow ceramic basin sat beside it.

A muffled sound from the hall drew her attention before the door opened. Robert appeared, his plaid draped around his hips, his chest bare. In his hands and arms was a bounty of food and a wineskin. He held a fierce expression, brows drawn together as he focused on holding all the items steady while he shoved the door shut with a hip. His gaze instantly softened when he caught her watching him, and he smiled. She moved to help him, but he shook his head.

"Stay there a moment, Susanna."

She did as he asked, watching from below the foot of the bed as he spread the feast out over the bedcovers. He went over to the wash basin, poured water over a fresh linen square, and held it between his hands as he walked over to her.

"Spread your legs for me," he said.

She blushed at his words, the gruffness in his voice and his furrowed brow catching her off guard. She bent her knees and eased her thighs apart, looking up at him all the while.

Had she realized only for the first time earlier today that Robert was handsome? He'd suddenly grown even more attractive to her. Two shining braids at his temple held his raven-black hair off his face, but it fell forward as he bent over her. His prominent cheekbones and dark brows had always given him a harsh quality, but now they were beautiful to her. Those full lips . . . oh what the man could do with those lips . . .

"I dinna hurt you too badly, did I?" he asked, his voice softening. With care, he cleansed her, wiping the cloth over parts that indeed were tender to the touch.

"Nay," she replied, smiling as warmth bloomed in her chest. "'Twas the most amazin' thing, Robert."

He left the cloth beside her and gazed at her naked form. To her surprise, she hadn't wanted to cover her bared body. Perhaps, although she'd escaped on her own, she'd now been set free. Robert had done that for her.

"Come, we must keep your energy up. I've surely worn you out." He took both of her hands into his and pulled her up from the bearskin.

The bed's enormous size amazed her; she'd been relegated to a tiny cot her whole life, her Mama given a narrow bed. This bed was three of each put together. The bedchamber itself was a palace compared to the cramped quarters they'd had to live in.

With the aromatic banquet Robert had brought, the luxurious bed with its silken sheets, and accommodations fit for a king, she felt spoiled. In the company of a man like she'd never in all her life expected, she felt blessed.

Robert pulled back the coverings, and she climbed under, the crisp coolness of the sheets shooting chills through her body. He removed his plaid and joined her under the covers.

"What're your favorite foods, Susanna? I dinna know what to bring, so I stole a wee bit of everythin'."

She grinned wide. "You brought all of this for *me?*"

Robert leaned over, staring into her eyes before kissing her tenderly. His lips brushed along her jaw up to her ear. He murmured, "Aye, love. I'd slay a dragon if you wanted just one scale."

"Mmm . . ." She leaned into his enchanting touch.

As he shifted toward the foot of the bed, she scanned over her choices. The end of a fragrant loaf of braided rosemary bread lay on one end, and she pulled off a small piece and popped the herbed morsel into her mouth.

Two kinds of cheeses, one hard and the other softer, sat beside a bowl of dark stewed cherries. He'd also brought a plum and a pear.

"What is this one?" She pointed to a pale orange, pear-shaped fruit.

"Quince." He halved the soft fruit with a dagger, sliced the inside into sections, and speared a piece, offering it to her.

She pulled the bite-sized piece off the blade and tried it. It had a mild, barely sweet flavor.

"And those?" She pointed to dark-brown, wrinkled fruits.

"Dates. A delicacy that tradin' . . . and raidin' . . . brought us from the Middle East." He plucked one up and held it before her. She wrapped her lips around the date, glancing at him as he watched her reaction with interest. Its unique nutty-sweet flavor filled her mouth.

"Where is the Middle East?" she asked as she chewed.

"'Tis a country far away, across the sea, in another part of the world. Crusaders brought back dates from their battles and travels. We had . . . an encounter . . . with them." He smirked. "We relieved them of many precious things that day."

She picked up another date between her fingers and offered it to him in the same manner.

He shook his head and scrunched his nose. "I doona like dates. Too sweet."

She tilted her head, examining a man she knew intimately, and yet, knew very little about. "Tell me what other things you doona like."

He picked up the wooden bowl full of stewed cherries, dragged his fingers through them, and held the tart fruit to her lips. She opened her mouth and wrapped her lips around his two fingers, sucking and licking them clean. He growled low, a look of mischief and desire flickering in his eyes.

"I can only think of everythin' I do like. Above all things I like and desire, one has risen to the top. You."

She blushed and looked away, the intensity of his gaze

heating her insides. She tore off and consumed another bite of bread, barely chewing, finding herself hungrier than she'd realized. He chuckled softly and picked up a wineskin, pulled out its cork, and handed it to her.

As she swallowed down the tart wine, Robert stifled a yawn. Unable to help herself, she pulled the flask from her lips, yawning unabashedly.

"Lie back, Susanna. Rest. We've had a long and eventful couple of days."

She slid further down on the bed and rested her head on one of the feathered pillows while Robert stood and transferred all the food to the table by the hearth. Her eyelids drifted closed as he settled beside her and tugged gently at her shoulder. She turned toward him on a sigh, nestling into his side, reveling in his immense warmth.

"And one incredible night," she murmured.

She drifted off to the feel of him pressing his lips to the top of her head as he whispered a tantalizing promise.

"'Tis the first in a lifetime of nights yet to come, my love."

Yet even in the warm protection of his embrace, menacing shadows hunted her in her dreams . . .

Sticky webs tasting of fear and malice sucked her under until she gasped for air, for freedom. Her father's maniacal bellow resonated into the nothingness, and she clamped her hands over her ears, terrified. Afraid to close her eyes, she stared as a foreboding silhouette materialized up a bleak stone wall, the snarling profile of a furious man seeking retribution.

Dougal.

His twisted shadow stretched taller, creeping onto the ceiling until it hovered over her, a specter threatening the nightmare of a torture worse than death.

She ran.

Chapter Eleven

Robert awoke to a constricting feeling. His eyelids popped open, and he launched away from something clutching his neck. But as he took in the foreign surroundings, he exhaled all the air in his lungs at a wonderful sight.

Sitting upright, an ivory sheet drifting off the curves of her breasts, was the most beautiful woman. *His* woman. Her hair was mussed from sleep, her cheeks were pinked, and her heavily lashed eyelids fluttered open then drifted shut again, as if the effort to see was too great.

"Robert? Is somethin' amiss?" she asked in a soft, sleepy voice.

"Nay. Not a thing." He smiled, and crawled beneath the covers once again. Susanna curled up into his side, yawning against his chest.

"I dinna sleep well. I had bad dreams I canna seem to remember." She tightened the arm she'd stretched across his chest for a brief moment before relaxing.

He rubbed his hand up and down her back, soothing her. The gentle creature he held in his arms may have had a dark past, but he swore her present and future would be filled with light. To carry out his endeavor, he needed to learn more about her.

"Susanna, tell me about your mother," he said, cringing as he heard the words, hoping the topic wouldn't change her sleepy, pliable demeanor.

Instead, she pressed closer against him, wrapping an arm around his chest and holding him tight. He sighed, thrilling over her possessiveness.

"Mama was the gentlest of souls. Givin', no matter who received what she offered. Forgivin' and lovin'," she said, her voice growing softer.

"She's no longer . . . *here* . . . is she." What started as a question fell flat into a statement. He knew. The fighter beneath her delicate exterior never would've left behind her beloved mother, the one person in the world, it seemed, who'd shown her kindness and love.

"Nay." Susanna's voice cracked.

Warm tears fell onto his chest and tracked down the side of his ribs. He made no move to stop the flow, only squeezed her shoulder in support.

"I doona know all that happened. Only that . . . he . . . called for her in the middle of the night. He did so often. She'd always returned before sunrise. That time . . . she never returned.

"When I demanded to see her, he led me down to the chapel. Dressed in a gown of white I'd never seen before, she lay upon a long table as if sleepin'. Her eyes were closed and her hands had been folded across her chest.

"Everythin' I'd held dear and sacred in my world vanished the moment Mama left this Earth. She knew it would happen. Although he never lifted a hand to me, he did to her. He'd made certain no marks showed, but she'd come back battered and bruised beneath her clothin'."

Robert exhaled a puff of air, disgusted by the knowledge that anyone would treat another soul with such hatred and disregard. "Susanna, I'm verra sorry." He tightened his grip on her.

She took a deep breath. "She made me promise that when she died—*not if, but when*—I was to leave the verra same night. I followed her instructions, takin' nothin' with me but a horse from the stables and enough food to make it to safety, wherever and however far away that happened to be."

"You nearly ran me down, gettin' there," he quipped,

smirking.

She gave a soft laugh and sniffled. "I dinna mean to, and yet, it turned out to be the most wonderful thing that ever happened to me."

Staying within his embrace, she shifted onto an elbow and gazed up at him. Her cheeks were shiny from her tears, her dark lashes stuck together from the wetness. "You are a wish I made. The verra thing I'd prayed for."

Robert smiled and leaned forward. With tender care, he kissed away the salty tears from her lashes as she fluttered them shut. He brushed back a few strands of hair that had stuck to her wet cheek and, with gentle reverence, did his best to kiss all her pain away.

"Thank you for nearly tramplin' me, threatenin' my life, and for bein' a feisty *guest* of ours. Were it not for your impossible nature, I might not have fallen for you."

"Guest?" she said, pulling her head back. "Doona you mean to say 'prisoner'?"

He laughed, kissing her luscious lips. He murmured against them between lazy kisses. "Nay, no matter who was the one bound, 'twas I who'd been captured."

She pulled back, staring into his eyes with great intensity. "Robert, I canna stop worryin' about my father and Dougal. They will come after me. You and your clan are at risk as long as I remain here. And . . ."

Robert swallowed hard, wanting to ease her suffering, but forcing himself to wait and listen to her needs. Her fear was justified and existed because, in the heat of battle, he'd chosen to protect her first and bring the fight to Dougal another time. On his terms. Without Susanna. He accepted the responsibility of easing her fears and worries until he killed Dougal. *And* her abusing, tyrannical father.

She slid her quivering fingers across his cheeks. "I'm tryin' desperately to trust you. Trust this. *Us*. Mama told me things. Made me believe things that I'm now fightin' against."

"What kind of things did she tell you, Susanna?"

"Horrible things about men. *All* men. I've grown up fearin' and hatin' men. I hated you the moment I met you. I knew no other way."

He turned his head, placing a gentle kiss in the palm of her hand. "And now?"

"Now I feel something verra different than hate for you, no matter my struggles with it."

His soft laugh brought a small smile to her lips. "Your bravery and strength is admirable after all you've been through. That you fight your demons and try to trust somethin' you never imagined possible is enough for now." He smiled at her. "I'm a verra patient man."

Susanna threaded her fingers through the hair at his nape and pulled him closer. He wrapped his arms around her, holding his new wife—his life.

Robert spent the entire morning in Susanna's bed, holding and reassuring her, but also talking with her and learning about little things, like the secret hikes she'd taken alone and the colorful wildflowers she'd discovered while on them. The moment springtime arrived, he planned to share many new small adventures with her.

The castle's daily activities were well underway by the time he ventured downstairs to replenish their food and drink. Maids were already clearing dishes from the day's first meal off the tables and tossing scraps to the hounds as he bounded down the stairs. He stepped into the cool space of the larder to refill their wineskin.

When he passed back by the kitchen, Iain called out to him. "Robert! Look at you, hale and well rested." A huge grin stretched across his face.

Robert narrowed his eyes, wary of Iain's sudden jovial demeanor. "Iain, you've been heavily drinkin' the ale already?"

"Nay." Iain held up the aromatic brew of what he and Isobel drank. They called it coffee.

Iain continued to stare at him with a devilish smirk on his face.

Robert growled low. "What's got you so *happy* today?"

He arched a brow. "I've called the priest. We heard you took a wife last night, and Father John *will* be givin' you God's blessin'."

Robert snorted. "You heard?"

"I doona think even the mice were spared Susanna's screams in the night. Damn, Robert. The walls are made of thick stone. I'd ask what you did to the poor lass, but it looks like she marked you in return." Iain clapped him hard on the shoulder and left the room.

Robert grabbed a silver tray and held it up by the light of the fire. Small bruises dotted the side of his neck from his shoulder to his jaw. He slowly smiled.

"Aye," he said aloud in the empty kitchen. "She marked me. Straight through to my heart."

His grin faltered as he stared at the irrefutable image of who he was: a warrior who'd stolen a bride from another man—a man who would die by the blade of his claymore. And he might be Susanna's husband by law, but he needed to explain the magick within their castle and how it affected their lives. He believed nothing should be kept secret between a husband and wife.

His dark brow furrowed in the reflection, and his jaw tensed as he replaced the platter on the table. After everything had been dealt with, and all had been revealed, he hoped she'd want to stay with him, be a part of Clan Brodie.

The celebrating would be tempered until he'd earned the right to keep her.

Chapter Twelve

After a lazy afternoon talking and laughing with Brigid and Isobel, and the last hour of their fussing over her hair and gown, Susanna sent her new friends down ahead of her and now descended the steps alone. The brief respite granted her valuable minutes alone to think about her situation. Although she'd spent the prior night in Robert's arms as he made her his, and spent the rest of the morning soaking in the warmth and protection of her warrior wrapped around her, it still hadn't settled completely into her mind that she'd given herself to a man.

I've been handfasted.

Mama had prepared her for the inevitable day that her father would sentence her to the fate of marriage. Nothing had readied her for what had happened though. She'd willingly chosen to be with a man, to belong to Robert.

Unaware in the heat of passion that the act itself would legally bind them, she'd given in to what her body . . . and her heart . . . had wanted. Only after her head had cleared, and he'd left her to her solitude, had his words sunk in. They'd become man and wife by the laws of the land.

Did she regret it? She had no idea.

As she tried to analyze whether she could stay here, rising terror threatened her ability to breathe. Mama had instilled within her a deep-seated need to seek her freedom at the first opportunity—to take control of her own fate, rather than relinquish it to the will of a man. Even this bright-spirited castle was no different than the last. Both had confining walls with men inside. And Robert's assurances of her safety did nothing to quell her fears of the evil still chasing her on the outside.

As she tried to imagine a new life within Clan Brodie, worry about an uncertain future overrode her concerns about the past. With each step down into the great hall, she felt a growing weight on her chest. Panic fluttered into her stomach about everything she didn't know. What would he expect of her? Where would they live? How often would he be away to lead his clansmen . . . and what would she do here while he was gone?

Were they *her* clansmen now too?

Midway down the steps, Susanna spotted Robert. His gaze locked onto her, and a grin spread wide across his face. She smiled in return as warmth bloomed in her chest, lifting the constriction she'd felt only a moment ago. Her head spun at how Robert's charm calmed her so completely.

With swift grace, he crossed the room and met her before her foot left the bottom step. The toes of her satin slippers never hit the main floor, because he swept her into his arms, and she squealed as he crushed the air from her lungs with his embrace.

"Robert!" She gasped for breath. "Put me down," she said with a soft laugh.

Light as air, she drifted down in his arms. His fingers laced into hers as he pulled her arms wide. "Susanna, you're a vision."

She blushed, glancing down at the ivory satin dress trimmed with tiny beads that glittered. It resembled the gown her mama last wore, as if it were a gift sent from Heaven for her.

"Thank you, Robert."

He tucked her against his side and led her into the room. "Come, we've a clan for you to meet."

Everyone's eyes were upon them, and there were nearly a hundred people in the large room, maybe more. She shrunk into his embrace, unaccustomed to the spotlight; she'd spent her life disappearing into the shadows.

"Doona be afraid, they're as anxious as you," Robert whispered.

She laughed. "I doona think that true at all. Why are we needin' to do this? 'Tis not true we're handfasted?"

"Aye, 'tis true, but Iain insists upon our clan witnessin' our union blessed before God," he replied.

"Oh." Another flicker of apprehension tripped down her spine. She slipped her hand into his larger one to ward the uneasiness away.

Robert's men, all dressed in their finest linen shirts and tartans, stared at them with interest, but she also saw a gleam of pride in their eyes. Toward Robert, she assumed. Many of the women, however, glared at her with undisguised hostility.

"Robert, do the women dislike me?"

He gripped her tighter into his side, and she glanced up to catch his chin drop, a single black brow arching. "Aye, and let them. They coveted me like a prize, but not one of them cared about the man beneath. All they can see is my physical vitality and my rank as commander."

The idea anyone wouldn't appreciate such an incredible man for who he truly was angered her, and she glared right back at them. Three of the worst offenders discontinued their staring, and instead began whispering among themselves. Her stomach clenched at the blatant animosity, and she gripped Robert's hand tighter. He rubbed a thumb over the back of her hand, and the simple gesture soothed away her agitation.

Robert guided her through the crowd until they stood before a man with short light-brown hair. He wore a white linen robe with a crimson over-tunic and a narrow, leather belt loose at his waist.

"Father John, this is Susanna."

"Most delighted to meet you, my dear," he said, bowing his head. "Let us proceed, shall we?"

Susanna looked around, surprised the event would begin the moment they arrived, but everyone in the room continued to look their way, conversations quieting.

Robert took both her hands in his, his dark eyes sparkling with joy. Susanna smiled up at him. He smiled broadly and gave her hands a gentle squeeze, and she exhaled, calming.

"We have come together tonight to celebrate a most happy occasion. Our beloved Robert has found himself a woman he approves of," the priest said.

The entire room roared with laughter. Robert growled low. "Doona taunt me, Father. Get on with it."

"Right, right," the priest replied, drawing his brows together, appearing more serious. He leaned in toward them. "What clan do you come from, my child?"

She stiffened. No part of her wanted to claim her heritage—she'd rejected them. Her blood ties had grown icy cold.

Robert gave a quick squeeze to her hands, and replied for her. "She's come to us sent from God, Father. Surely that is good enough."

The priest's eyes widened and he smiled. He cleared his throat as the crowd's laughter from his first words died down.

"God has sent us the bonnie Susanna to be wed to Robert of the clan Brodie. It is in love that two strengthen, united as one. We are here to witness their profession before the clan and in the eyes of God.

"Do you, Susanna, take Robert to be your husband, honoring and loving him for all the days of your life?"

Susanna smiled, gazing up into her warrior's eyes. "I do."

"Robert, do you take Susanna to be your wife, cherishing and protecting her?"

"Aye. And honorin' . . . and lovin' . . ."

Robert's eyes smoldered at his profession, and Susanna felt a flush heat her skin from the neck up. She took a deep breath, remembering exactly how he loved . . .

"Then by the power of God I pronounce the two of you *officially* husband and wife."

Robert's hands flew to her back, and he lifted her up in his arms, his lips crushing against her mouth. She flung her arms around his neck and surrendered to the passionate kiss, a tiny moan escaping her throat. He broke their kiss before they got carried away, but groaned as if he couldn't bear their separation. She laughed, feeling a bit more at ease with the entire situation.

As if on cue, servants burst out of the kitchen, one after another, lining up platters of food onto the tables before circling back and bringing more.

Iain and Isobel approached, bringing silver goblets of ale, one in each of their hands.

"Congratulations, Robert." Iain handed Robert a drink and then gave her a broad grin. "Welcome to our family, Susanna."

Isobel handed her the fourth goblet. They raised them high, and Susanna did the same, holding the narrow base between her fingers.

"May your life be blessed with abundant love and your house with many bairns," Iain said, pulling Isobel into his side.

Susanna lifted her glass, and then put her lips to the rim, sipping on the mellow honeyed ale. Her mind spun with all the events, and most recently, Iain's words. Love. Babies. Two days ago she hadn't given a single thought to her life having either.

The notion that the veering of her horse in one particular direction over any other had led her to this point amazed her. Perhaps God *had* delivered her here, and her holding the reins had all been for show.

"Robert," she whispered, "where exactly is *our* house?"

"I . . . *we* have a cottage within the curtain wall. 'Tis the one closest to the stables and smithy, but also nearest to the stream and garden. While not as luxurious as your bedchamber here, 'tis verra comfortable."

She briefly thought of the cramped quarters she'd grown up in. Whatever Robert felt comfortable in, she had no doubt she would too. "'Twill be perfect, Robert."

He smiled and nuzzled his lips into her temple. "*You're* perfect, Susanna."

Chills raced down her side from his touch, yet warmth from deep within her chest spread everywhere from his words. She leaned into him as the dizzying combination made her footing feel unstable.

In front of them, Iain took Isobel's hand, looping it into his arm as he guided her toward the head of the table. Robert placed a firm hand in the small of her back, urging her forward to follow them. But the bevy of jealous women stood directly in their way.

Susanna squared her shoulders and notched her head higher. She felt Robert's hand rub up and down once on her back, the support bolstering her courage.

The aggressive women parted for them without a word, but another woman, not from the threesome, approached her right before they sat down. She had pale blond hair and kind blue eyes.

"Forgive me for staring before," she said. "I was only surprised that Robert had chosen a woman ... an English woman ... to be his wife. I'm Donalda." She nodded in respect.

"'Tis verra nice to meet you, Donalda. You're mistaken, though. Mama may have been English, but since my entire life has happened in Scotland, I suppose I'm no more English than any of you."

The woman stepped closer to her, whispering in her ear, "Those three are burrs in everyone's side. They've focused on Robert so long, 'tis caused them to lose sight of the other worthy men in our clan. Given time, they'll find other pastimes to occupy their attention. They do have a mighty sting when angered though. You'd do well to give them room."

"Thank you for the warnin', Donalda. I hope they each find what they're lookin' for."

"Aye. We all do. I'm not sure the clan can survive another year of their schemes and gossip." Donalda snorted. She turned to leave, but gently grasped Susanna's forearm. "Doona worry overly much. Iain won't stand for people bein' intolerant. We're a clan, bound to protect and love one another, and he reminds us when warranted." She bowed her head then rushed off to take a seat at the far table.

Robert leaned down. "She's right, love. Iain will put a

quick end to unhealthy behavior in the clan. That's if I doona have the chance to first."

Regardless of Donalda and Robert's assurances, the men had greater battles to fight than hers. But she didn't understand their aggression toward her, when Robert clearly had rejected the lot. She wondered if it was something more. Perhaps she spoke more like her mother than she'd thought. "Do I seem that English?"

Robert helped guide her down onto the bench. "Nay, only a wee bit. You've a small English accent to some of your words, but much less so than Lady Isobel. We've all grown used to her ... *slang*." Robert winked across the table at Isobel.

"Ha!" Isobel replied, laughing. "I'll have you speaking my *slang* in no time."

Robert sighed. "Somethin' we've all been secretly afraid of."

They all laughed, a light-hearted atmosphere permeating the room, and she started to breathe easier. Iain began helping Isobel and himself to the food, and everyone did the same. Even Susanna had grown bolder overnight, lifting her plate without delay for servings of whatever Robert dished out for them.

In the hall's decorated wonderland, laughter accompanied personal stories and commentary. She quietly ate beside her new husband among a clan that, for the vast majority, seemed like a protective, tight-knit family. The atmosphere was far different from any meals she'd witnessed growing up—tense and focusing on the next battle to conquer the weak or ill-deserving. Even the unwelcoming women had distanced themselves and engaged in bright banter among their friends. Perhaps Donalda was right—given time they *would* accept the loss of Robert.

Jovial chatter faded as a bard joined in the celebration, sitting beside the hearth, opposite the Christmas tree. He regaled them with tales of heroics in the age of King Arthur as he plucked the strings of a lyre with his right hand, his left securing it upon a knee.

The bard shared versions of the fabled adventures she'd

not heard before. With the amount of good spirits in the room, that they cast stories in a brighter light didn't surprise her. Her past, *her former clan*, merely happened to be darker than most, she decided. Surrounded by the protective clan, her new family, she realized she could do what she had vowed to do before this clan and God. For the first time, she began to believe that she could embrace forever with a man.

A sudden crash directly across the table snapped her attention forward. Brigid had slammed her plate down, sending her food flying across the table.

"Brigid, I feel him, too. Leave it be." Isobel warned her friend.

Susanna looked between the two women, uncertain what the provocation was about.

"Nay." Brigid growled and stood. "My appetite is gone." Brigid looked at her and Robert, giving them a tight smile. "I'm verra happy for the two of you. Please ignore my irritable mood and enjoy your meal."

Susanna's heart clenched for Brigid when Isobel intimated the cause of her unknown distress was a *him*. She opened her mouth to console her, but adequate words never came as she silently watched Brigid turn and disappear down the shadowed hall. All the while, the bard sang and played his music, and everyone carried on their conversations, oblivious to the trouble at the head of their table.

"Weel, you heard her, you two. Eat," Robert said.

Susanna turned to find Robert glancing between her and Isobel with arched brows. He waited until she put a large bite of pheasant in her mouth before his heated stare eased and he continued eating.

"Lady Isobel, tell us more of your Christmas," Robert said.

"Oh, let's see," Isobel began. "*My* Christmas was nothing like the grandeur of what Clan Brodie now has; we had no snow. Beaches, sunshine, and buying a Christmas tree in a mall parking lot were my experiences."

"Isa," Iain chided. "Tell them of what an ideal Christmas would be. Embrace your inner storyteller."

They finished their meal to Isobel's stories of families at Christmas spending time together in celebration—much like their joyous occasion tonight—and strayed to stranger topics like carolers going door to door, Secret Santas, and something about a white elephant gift at a university. While the handful still at their end of the table talked, more than half the people in the room had taken to dancing, the bass sounds of a large drum and the chords of a lute creating a lively rhythm.

Susanna's mind, however, lingered on all the curious things Isobel had shared. Based on the colorful descriptions, she understood carolers to be a group of bards bringing songs of cheer to people's homes, and Secret Santas was a game of gifts where the identity of the giver was unknown. She had no idea what a mall parking lot was, or a university, or . . .

"What is an *elephant?*" Susanna asked, glancing beyond Isobel's shoulder at a dancing couple who swung wildly around and around to the squealing lass's delight.

Isobel's brow furrowed. "Oh," she said quietly. Isobel glanced at Iain as her mouth fell open, wordlessly.

"Doona look at me, Isa. You started this Christmas affair. 'Tis all on you," Iain said, smirking.

"Well, a white elephant gift is what we call it when—" Isobel's eyes dropped to the table. She stared at the heavily grained wood before lifting to meet her gaze again "—we play a game with presents . . ."

"And an elephant?" Susanna asked again.

Iain chuckled.

Isobel sighed. "It's a very large animal . . . from another continent . . . ah . . . country."

"Bigger than a bear?" Robert asked.

"Yes. Bigger than a bear," Isobel replied. "It stands taller than two bears atop one another and is about the size of six or seven bears put together."

"Och, you jest!" Robert said.

"Nay," Iain interjected. "She speaks the truth."

Robert laughed and tugged Susanna up. "Come, Susanna, I want to dance with my bride."

She stood into the strong grip of his arms. His

captivating scent wrapped around her as she looked up into
his eyes.

Such a strange thing, to be held by a man.

Dark and more deadly than any man she'd known,
Robert's very existence made her wonder at the quick turn of
recent events. How could Mama not have told her that *some*
men were capable of kindness and love? Had Mama's papa
been a tyrant, too? Had she never known of a man like
Robert? Surely she couldn't have, else she would've
mentioned the difference.

As Robert pulled her toward the center of the wooden
floor, a piercing crash echoed from beyond the room. They all
turned toward the kitchen as another loud clang, a
resounding clatter, and a tinkling smash echoed out from
beyond the shadowed doorway.

Five people burst from the kitchen, fleeing in various
directions.

"Oh, hell," Isobel said loud enough for the entire room to
hear.

Iain scowled and sprang up from the bench, glaring at
the commotion, but Isobel laid a hand on his forearm to stop
him, imperceptibly shaking her head.

Something smaller shattered, its sound half that of the
one before. Susanna tore her eyes from the direction of the
disturbance and stared at Iain and Isobel, who apparently
knew the reason for all the destruction.

The deafening crash of a much larger object rang out
from the kitchen, and the musicians finally stopped playing,
all conversations ceasing.

"I guess she couldn't leave it alone," Isobel muttered, her
tone somber.

"You lied!" Brigid's shouted accusation came from the
unseen battlefield of the kitchen followed by her growl of
frustration that escalated to a high-pitched scream.

Suddenly, a shiny object spiraled into the room and
smashed into the stone wall beside the Christmas tree,
shattering into tiny glittering fragments before they rained
down in sparkles. A low-timbered, masculine voice rumbled
from the vicinity of the battle, but the words were

indecipherable. Susanna swallowed hard, trepidation quickening her heart, her mind racing over the distraught Brigid and the man at the root of her anguish.

Robert pushed Susanna back with an extended arm, moving them both away from the danger. A large platter sailed through the air and hit the same exact spot before it too exploded into pieces.

"She has superb aim," Robert remarked.

Susanna snorted, more from nervousness than amusement. She'd never seen a woman more enraged, other than herself.

Another growl from the kitchen turned into shouted unintelligible words. More crashing and shattering happened for an extended period of time to a completely silent great hall.

Robert's gaze flew to Iain, and he took a step toward his laird. Susanna surmised Robert's first instinct was to protect his clan, even if it was from one another.

Iain shook his head, setting his jaw and clenching it. "My furious sister seems to have broken every piece of glass we've acquired."

Robert stayed his action, waiting. Everyone else did the same. With the tension in the great hall growing nearly as thick as the battle in the kitchen, no one dared utter a word.

Brigid burst from the kitchen, her copper hair flying in a blaze around her head as she rushed through the room in a blur. The standing crowd shrank out of her way, parting out of instinct and self-preservation.

Fast on her heels, the dark angel stormed after her, his scowl far surpassing the one Brigid wore. The glare in his shining eyes threatened to set the rest of the world on fire. Susanna had no doubt he could.

Beside Robert, Father John stepped forward, far too close to the path of danger. The man of God gaped at the dark, winged creature as if he confronted a hound from hell, and he crossed himself. Twice.

Skorpius glared at Father John as he passed him, those astounding black wings arching up higher. "Not. One. Word. *Priest.*"

The angel shot a searing look Robert's direction, as if Robert would be the next to challenge him, and Susanna swore she felt the scorching heat of the creature's glare. Robert, however, remained where he stood, unflinching.

Skorpius never broke stride. His arrival and departure happened in a few of the rapid heartbeats that thundered in Susanna's ears.

Total silence lingered in the wake of the mayhem. No one moved.

Susanna realized she'd forgotten to breathe and sucked in a lungful of air. At witnessing another woman suffer at the hands of a man, a cold familiar fear licked up into her heart, freezing all the warmth until a chill racked through her body.

Iain addressed the priest in a surprisingly calm tone from where he remained at the table. "Pray for us, Father. Pray our dear Brigid doesn't kill that angel before I've had a chance to. And pray to God Brigid dinna toss the silver plates and goblets into the ovens."

Isobel burst into laughter, along with the room. The tension-filled crowd needed the unexpected release. The humor didn't reach Susanna, though. She did her best to breathe through her escalating terror.

"Iain, help me up. I'm going after her," Isobel said.

"The *hell* you are," he growled.

Isobel patted his arm as she rose, and Iain helped her in spite of his crass reply.

"Iain, I'll be fine. This isn't a dark back alley in Los Angeles. It's our home. That isn't a hardened criminal going to jump me. It's Skorpius. Remember, he saved your life and this clan. Do find a way to have confidence in my judgment."

Iain sighed and gave his wife a heavy look but said no more. She kissed Iain's cheek and went off down a darkened corridor.

"I'm goin', too," Susanna whispered to Robert. She needed to see Brigid, to prove to herself the fiery woman hadn't suffered physical harm.

Robert grasped her forearm as she stepped away. "Susanna . . ."

"Robert, I must. Brigid's now my friend too." She stared

down the corridor as Isobel disappeared from view, desperately needing the comfort only another woman could give her.

He released her arm, and she didn't look back; the rising panic in her chest commanding her very effort to breathe.

As she rushed after them, fragments of statements and events crisscrossed through her mind until everything tangled together. Her pulse raced as she ran, heartrending memories of Mama's distress at the hands of her father flooding her mind.

Along the dark corridor, a pool of yellow light shimmered, cast from a torch in an iron fitting. She pressed into the unknown darkness from the small comfort of the light, alarmed by the confusing thoughts spinning in her head: Iain mentioned her being imprisoned here; Brigid had been upset by the angel, who wasn't a man, but was clearly male—and had hurt Brigid; and Robert had been possessive with her from the moment they'd met, took her body as if it had been fated, and authoritatively claimed that she belonged to him. Now she did belong. In marrying him, she'd become another man's possession. Yet they'd not truly argued about anything of consequence. Would he show his true colors, proving himself to be like all other men, if they vehemently disagreed?

She paused in the middle of the hall in the darkness, willing herself to breathe as pins and needles spread through her chest and the floor tilted. After a few moments, the nauseous feeling passed, and she continued, spurred onward by the quiet conversation drifting down the corridor.

"I'm *happy* he's gone." Brigid's tortured sob echoed off the stone walls. "Vanished into thin air like Fingall. Like the *children*."

"I know, Brigid. I've no idea why any of those things happened. The rules of his world make no sense in ours, yet we suffer the price of their puzzling actions, regardless."

A heavy sigh was followed by a stuttered hiccup. Brigid murmured a string of unintelligible words.

"I wish I could do something to make your pain go away," Isobel replied softly.

Pain? Is Brigid injured? Susanna's lungs knotted again.

When she rounded the next corner, Isobel and Brigid were huddled in each other's arms in another golden pool of torchlight. They glanced up as she approached. Tracks of tears ran down Brigid's face, but she made no move to wipe them away. A quick glance over her body showed no visible marks. But experience told Susanna clothing hid many things.

Oh, sweet heavens, she needed to make peace with her mind. Needed to know how to discover the truth, and once and for all, put her fears to rest if they were truly unfounded.

"Are you hurt, Brigid? I couldn't bear it if he'd harmed you." She stepped closer.

"Nay," Brigid said, resignation coloring her voice. "I'm sorry I've upset you, Susanna. He dinna harm me physically. And he dinna abuse me emotionally. Not directly anyway."

No matter what Brigid said, Susanna's heart refused to stop thundering. Her hands shook so badly, she buried them into the folds of her dress and focused on a seam in the stone floor while she tried to slow her breaths.

"Susanna, talk to us," Brigid said, standing taller. "I dinna think about how my uproar would distress you. Please forgive me."

Susanna exhaled slowly, steadying her riotous nerves in small measure while her heart hurt for her friend. "I . . . Brigid I'm verra sorry for whatever he's done. 'Tis the wrong time, I know . . . but—"

Nervous, she clasped her hands, wringing them. She'd never asked anyone for anything before. The proper way to go about it escaped her knowledge, and she felt suddenly inadequate.

Isobel placed a gentle hand on her shoulder.

Brigid shook her head and gave her a weak smile. "Go on, Susanna. *Please.* I need a distraction to calm down."

Distraction. Susanna looked at the gray stone floor of the corridor and took a fortifying breath. She glanced back up at her two friends, focusing beyond the frightening thoughts in her mind and the thunderous pulse in her ears.

Although trust was new and fleeting for her, she had to

believe these women would trust what she was about to tell them, and she had to convince Robert that she felt fine when she returned to him for their wedding night. Despite the real-life threats to her person and their clan, with the inescapable demons haunting her mind, her very sanity depended on it.

"I need your help."

Chapter Thirteen

Robert remained where he stood when Susanna last left him, his gaze locked onto the dark corridor down which she'd disappeared. The concern on her face had been understandable, but it was the panic in her eyes that distressed him. He hoped that Brigid and Isobel would soothe Susanna's fears about those things *most unbelievable* within his clan. Things he'd intended to explain tonight, before fate once again commanded otherwise.

With events happening on pace like the very winds of the blizzard that had blown her here, he still hadn't had the time to explain to her about the magick Brodie Castle held—or the fantastical events often occurring because of it—but he would. Perhaps in support of what Brigid and Isobel might reveal.

He raked his hand through his unbound hair and took a deep breath to calm his rising nerves. The corridor leading to the castle's ancillary rooms had never looked so desolate.

A tankard of ale appeared before his face. "Doona fret about the lasses. All problems with women have a way of workin' themselves out. Trust me."

He glanced at Iain and took the offered drink. After half a dozen hearty swallows, he took another calming breath and nodded. "I've never had to handle a woman before," he admitted.

Iain roared in laughter. "You've handled plenty, my

friend. But this is the one who sets your head spinnin' and your heart racin', and handlin' her requires care and patience."

Robert snorted. "Aye."

Susanna suddenly appeared at the far side of the room, accompanied by her newfound friends. They all looked stronger than they had when they'd left, and three more bonnie lasses he'd never seen. Isobel walked on the left with her wavy blond hair; Brigid on the right with her wild red curls; and in the middle, with an arm looped into each of theirs, was Susanna, her raven locks gently framing a most angelic face.

Susanna caught his gaze and smiled, which made her all the more stunning. His chest ached, as if her look of happiness had taken hold of his heart and squeezed. He strode across the room, unable to stop himself. The women beside her each brushed a kiss to Susanna's cheeks and drifted away from her side, into the crowded room.

He tried to still his shaking hands as he took her delicate fingers in them, lifted them to his mouth, and placed a gentle kiss on each. "Susanna. I worried when you'd run off. There are many things I need to tell you, to explain to you."

Her smile widened, and she lifted a finger, placing it on his lips. "Not tonight, Robert. Take me to bed."

He kissed the tip of her finger. "With great pleasure, wife," he replied, his voice husky.

Goodbyes and well wishes were shouted at their backs with laughter as he hoisted Susanna into his arms and raced up the stone steps. He paused halfway down the corridor, breathless, only to have her wind her hands around his neck and kiss him with body-melting heat. They passionately explored each other's mouths as he continued down the hall, a renewed urgency pumping through his veins.

Unable to see the latch to the door, he fumbled with the iron lever until it released, sending the heavy oak barrier flying open from their weight against it. He kicked a foot behind him, slamming the door shut with a loud thud.

They broke the kiss together, breathless and gazing deep into the other's eyes. Susanna knew him better than any other. He knew her better than he knew himself. Two lost souls, drifting through life, had collided, becoming one. He'd never felt more blessed.

With a shaky inhalation, he carefully placed her on her feet as they stood on the far side of the carved bed in front of the open window. Someone had tied back the bedchamber's tapestry, but the hearth's blazing fire sent ample warmth into the large room.

In gentle worship, he removed the delicate white layers of fabric from her body as she trembled beneath his fingers. Her gaze fell to the floor, and she blushed as if he hadn't touched her before. As his hands skimmed over her smooth curves, the silken chemise she'd worn beneath her gown drifted to the ground.

Her porcelain skin shimmered in the moonlight, luminous. When a burst of cool air danced bumps across her arms and chest, she shivered. He impulsively lifted his arms to warm her, but she grasped his forearms, staying his action.

"'Tis my turn." Her words were soft, but they held a tone of command.

He smiled and dropped his hand. "Aye. My body is yours."

Susanna tilted her head, a faraway look appearing in her eyes before she focused on him again. She lifted her fingers to the pin fastening his plaid and released the silver clasp with a tug. The woolen fabric unraveled, falling to the ground. With her sparkling eyes locked onto his, she pulled up his linen shirt, and he raised his arms in assistance as she dragged the material over his head.

Her soft hands fluttered over his chest and drifted down over his abdomen. Each of his muscles tensed in reaction to her warm touch no matter how he tried to relax. She paused in her descent, placing a gentle kiss over the linen bandage covering his wound.

His heart hammered dents into the backside of his ribs as her fingertips drifted lower and teased across each of his hips. His cock twitched, throbbing and aching for her touch. Deep breaths and tremendous focus were the only things that kept him standing—and his hands and mouth restrained.

Her soft words purred heat over skin already on fire. "Aye, and what a fine body you have, Robert."

She sat down upon the bed, perched on the edge, as her eyes locked onto his bobbing shaft. He watched her in rapt fascination, unable to move. He swallowed hard, finding it difficult to breathe.

"I'm free to do anythin' I like?" she asked, her gaze flicking up to his.

He tried to answer, but his throat had locked up. A gravelly croak managed to break free. "Aye."

The woman actually smirked at him. Her gaze drifted back down his body to land on what stood at proud attention to her. *For her.*

"Any way I like?" She licked her lips.

"Aye," he whispered.

She extended her tongue. He stared down with held breath as she licked the underside of the tip. He hissed, sucking air in between his teeth.

Her eyes widened as his cock twitched, hardening further, throbbing mercilessly. She wrapped her fingers around the base of the shaft and tightened her grip as she placed her lips at the tip and pulled him inside. He groaned, closing his eyes.

Delivering pleasure-filled torture, she slowly licked and sucked. He trembled under her attention, tightening his thighs and calves to prevent his body from collapsing to the floor. For a woman unfamiliar with a man's body, his wife had great intuition on what pleased him.

Her other hand drifted up the inside of his thigh. Caresses, licks, sucks—she leisurely explored his body, satisfying her curiosity, teasing his last threads of control, of which he had only a tenuous hold.

When she moaned low—his cock deep in her mouth and her hands cupping and lifting—he growled. His hand dropped to her jaw, urging her back with a gentle pressure, not wanting her to bite down in surprise. On a slow, long suck, she pulled her mouth off of him, a popping sound echoing into the room as she finally released the engorged tip.

She looked up at him, smiling. "You enjoyed my mouth on you?"

His breaths came out in short bursts, ragged and shallow. The woman had pulled him right to the edge of release.

"Aye. Back on the bed, Susanna. *My. Turn.*"

The moment she reclined, he stalked between her legs, forcing her back until she'd fallen onto the center of the bed. He settled his shoulders between her knees, pressing her soft thighs wide open. Delicate and pink, the very center of her glistened, sweet and ripe just for him. He swiped a flattened tongue through her folds.

Susanna moaned, squirming in his hold. He tightened his grip on her thighs, holding her immobile while he took his time to pleasure her, to tease her right to the brink, exactly as she'd done to him. He nipped with his teeth, soothed with soft kisses, tortured her in slow licks before he slid two fingers inside and stroked with gentle pressure. The erotic sounds she made, her shaky breaths, guided him in what she liked, what her body needed. She cried out, her thighs quivering as she grabbed the bedding in tightened fists.

A single pulse grasped his fingers tightly, and he slowed, holding her right below the breaking point. As he kept her there, she thrashed more, low whimpers escaping with her every exhalation. In slow measure, he teased her, ignoring his cock that had hardened to a near-painful degree.

"Robert . . ."

She moaned his name, and the sound was the sweetest wine, intoxicating.

"Robert . . . *Oh* . . . Robert . . . *please* . . ." Her words drifted into mumbled incoherency.

He ceased his actions, pulling away from her, needing her wrapped around him as much as she needed him deep within her. "Please *what*, my love?"

With patience, he kissed a trail up her body, his lips meandering up her quivering belly, stopping for a small suck of the delicate skin over her ribs. With his firm tongue, he licked beneath the swell of her breast and up, circling her nipple as the peaked tip hardened further. He captured it playfully between his teeth, tugging on it.

She speared her hands into his hair, pulling him forward. He released her breast and climbed higher.

Lust filled her eyes, dark blue and sparkling in the firelight. He nipped her lips, the tip of his cock fitting into her entrance.

Susanna arched, but his movement flowed with her, denying her what she needed.

She groaned, and he smiled, loving what he did to her. The woman, so sure of herself, independent and needing no one, came apart in his arms. In all his dreams, he'd have it no other way.

"Please what?" he repeated on a whisper, but kissed her again, preventing her reply.

Her hands slapped onto his hips, her fingernails digging into his ass as she pulled his body forward in demonstration. She arched again—the action pulling him a little deeper—as she threw her head back.

"Please . . . *please* take me," she begged.

Robert thrust forward, capturing her lips in a searing kiss. He groaned into her mouth as he plunged deep inside her welcoming body, intense pleasure sizzling through his nerve endings. He rocked back and pressed forward, over and over in a slow dance, as her cries grew. Unable to contain the fire raging through him, he lifted her hips and pumped into her with renewed force.

Liquid heat wrapped around him as a pulse fired from her, then another. In slow restraint, he continued the measured pace, a bead of sweat trickling down his forehead from the great effort. Susanna trembled and suddenly clutched his hips in a bruising hold. Fully seated deep inside of her, he stilled, sensing that she drifted onto the precipice— where he swayed, about to fall over the edge.

Susanna whimpered and arched her hips into him. He tightened his hold, lifting her ass higher. He flexed his hips hard, and she cried out. When he did it again, she dropped her head to his shoulder, releasing a sob into his skin as her entire body began to shake. Another deep thrust, and she screamed. Hard pulses gripped him as a wash of warmth flooded in, bathing him in her release.

He abandoned all restraint, pulling back and driving forward. Her cries magnified as his movements pulled marvelous sounds of found ecstasy from her throat. Intense pleasure unfurled from his spine, shot through his loins, and fired out hard and fast. He gasped from its force before his roar burst out into the room.

The world exploded into fragments of sensation, everything happening at once.

Heavy breaths.

Slickened skin.

Pounding hearts.

The logs in the hearth shifted, the fire crackling and snapping. A cool draft in the room prickled, rushing over his heated skin. Beautiful, trusting eyes gazed up at him, a small smile curving onto her glistening face.

"If God granted me a last piece of time to treasure forever, this would be it," she whispered.

He sighed, tears springing into his eyes as he was overcome by new emotions assaulting his heart. "Aye, love. This would be it."

Susanna wrapped her arms and legs around him as her lips nuzzled his neck, kissing the skin softly. He remained within her embrace, his hands tucked beneath her shoulders, his face buried in the sweet lavender scent of her hair, his body buried deep inside her.

For the first time in his life, *he* felt protected. Cherished. *Loved.*

Susanna shot upright in bed, gasping for breath as she escaped the suffocating clutches of another nightmare. Only this time, the vivid images burned into her memory, terrifying her. She glanced left to see Robert slumbering on his stomach, his back rising and falling in slow, steady breaths, his skin faintly illuminated by the last glowing embers in the hearth.

His amazing peace was completely at odds with her debilitating unrest. In her dreams, demons in Robert's likeness had chased her, threw flames at her until her lungs filled with choking smoke. Even awake, she couldn't breathe, undeniable fear of him transforming into that demon at some point in the future seizing her chest.

Acting on impulse, she quickly dressed and traipsed down the hall, counting the doors. She softly knocked on Brigid's. Torturous seconds later, the door opened to reveal her sleepy friend, copper curls a wild riot around her face.

"Susanna!" Brigid whispered, wrapping a robe over her sleeping gown. "Are you unwell?"

"Aye, at least in the head. My thoughts are jumbled with fears, and I canna breathe. I feel like my poundin' heart might explode out of my chest. I need that fresh air and time to think." They'd discussed her idea in the torch-lit corridor the night before, the possibility of a night ride.

Brigid nodded. "Meet me down in the great hall. I'll try to get Isobel away."

Both women appeared minutes later and spirited Susanna to the other end of the keep, through a gallery of Iain's collected treasures, and into the down-sloping entrance of a hidden tunnel. Isobel handed her a fiery torch she'd pulled from a fitting in the hall.

"I still don't think this is a good idea." Isobel repeated her misgivings from the night before.

Brigid wrapped a thick black cloak around Susanna's wedding dress. "Susanna promised it was only to think. And with *Solus* protectin' her, she'll be fine."

"Thank you. Both of you are so kind to me. Though you doona need to loan me your horse, my mare will do."

"No."

"Nay."

Isobel laughed at their simultaneous reply, but the smile faded, and she glared at Susanna. "You'll take my battle-trained horse, or we won't help you with the head-clearing ride you need. Understand?"

Susanna laughed, grateful for their help at all. "Aye."

She took her time wandering down into the airtight passage as she had the shortest distance to cover. The chilly corridor had been constructed large enough for her to stand upright and spread her arms wide before her fingertips grazed the tightly fitted stones on either side.

As she slowed her steps, she watched the shadows waver and creep along the walls and ceiling, bidden by her flickering torch. But she wasn't frightened. Only the dark corners of her tortured mind seemed to have that power.

A wooden ladder built into the wall appeared ahead, and she slid the torch into an iron fitting a few feet to its right. She took a deep breath, lifted her skirts, and carefully secured each slipper-covered foot into the rungs as she climbed out. As she rose toward the surface, colder air fogged down and around her until she pushed through thick scrub in front of the entrance and stepped out into the snow.

She pulled her borrowed cloak tightly around her as a biting wind whipped an icy frost into her bones. Ignoring the discomfort, she closed her eyes and slanted her face to the starry sky, inhaling the crisp cold air, the effects of the outside wilderness already calming her.

The sound of crunching snow alerted her moments before Brigid and Isobel walked into view, leading a regal mare whose white coat glowed in the light of the moon. That the two women would give her such a prized animal shocked her. Although they'd formed the fast bonds of friends and family, they'd still only known her for two days.

She was amazed by their kindness and generosity, but remembered Isobel's nonnegotiable terms. "I'll take good care of her."

"Aye, you will. And yourself." Brigid said. "Iain and Robert will be roarin' the castle down if harm comes to either of you."

"Are you certain we can't convince you to ride with Brigid tomorrow?"

Susanna shook her head. "Nay. I need to clear my head before I lose my mind. And I canna do so with company."

Warmth suddenly surrounded her, both women wrapping her in a fierce hug. She squeezed back, tears filling her eyes as she clung to two kindhearted souls that, in the best ways, reminded her of Mama.

Although she'd only shared with them brief details of Mama and her father, they had to be aware of Dougal's attack in the woods prior to her arrival. They honored her, both by not prying about something she wasn't able to talk about and in trusting her instincts that she'd be safe on a short midnight ride.

Nearly an hour later, Susanna rode Isobel's majestic horse through the snowy landscape, everything blurring together into the moonlit darkness. Tears in her eyes spilled over, tracking down hot across her cheeks in the biting wind. The stabbing cold on her skin and the choking cramp in her throat were far easier to bear than the crushing weight within her chest.

The nighttime ride meant to calm her head and lift her spirits, like other solitary rides had done, had the opposite effect. Head spinning and heart clenching, images of Robert and Dougal, Broc, and terrifying demons in very real nightmares haunted her until her breaths had reduced to ragged hitches and gulps of air. As pins and needles spread across her chest and down her arms, she focused on trying to breathe, her body forcing her to survive through her anxiety.

Thoughts ebbed away with the pins and needles as deep cold breaths filled her lungs. Numbness followed. Everywhere. And oddly, the absence of thought felt good. The farther *Solus* galloped from where Susanna had been, the less her fears ruled her mind.

Another salty tear tracked down her cheek as she realized her maddening thoughts had overruled good sense. *Solus* had charged off into the night without turning back. Lost in her fears and unaware of her surroundings, Susanna had foolishly let it happen. The boundary markers of Brodie lands that Isobel and Brigid had mentioned had disappeared into the dark of the early morning hour, unnoticed.

Her breath caught as reality settled into lucid thoughts. A part of her wanted to pull on the reins and urge *Solus* back to the castle, hoping the mare would find it. But the part of her frozen in terror from dark, twisted nightmares locked up her muscles.

Daunting fears, stalking her while awake and dreaming, thwarted her chance at happiness. Although she hadn't intended to leave, in her demon-haunted mind, she now saw no other way.

She had to abandon Robert. Her panic had reached such a degree within the confines of his castle, she had found it impossible to breathe. No matter what Robert promised, aside from whatever he truly believed, she would remain a prisoner in Brodie Castle—Iain had said as much himself.

Skorpius's transgression, whatever it had been—and the degree to which it had torn Brigid apart—only added to her growing fears. Seeing Brigid so forlorn had shredded her heart anew, ripping wide open the emotional scars from her past, proving to Susanna just how deep they ran. Broc may have physically hurt Mama, but the bruises she bore on the outside were mere scratches compared to the permanent damage Mama had sustained on the inside . . . that Susanna continued to suffer from.

She'd inadvertently escaped. Again. A lifetime of fears and her mother's words had coalesced into an undeniable need to run, even though a part of her knew that, in Robert and his clan, she'd found something truly rare and amazing. But although Susanna desperately wanted to believe her overwhelming panic was only temporary, she found she couldn't see even a flicker of light through the darkness of her despair.

Her frozen fingers gripped the reins hard, or she thought they did—she couldn't feel them anymore. She inhaled a deep shaky breath, wishing the painful beats of her heart would somehow grow numb as well.

A single sob escaped her throat. Flames ignited like wildfire from her chest into her throat as she attempted to hold the devastating emotions back. She failed. *Solus's* ears swiveled back, and the horse slowed, as she slumped over the mare's neck, crying.

Susanna hadn't felt comfortable bringing a location-marking torch to light her way, but the moon shone brightly enough for the horse to navigate unaided through the lightly treed area beyond Castle Brodie. Despite insurmountable fears that allowed for no other option but the choice she'd made, loneliness and sorrow plagued her mind. A wolf howled somewhere off in the distance as if commiserating with her—two miserable souls in the same place, both desolate and inconsolable.

She closed her eyes, trusting *Solus* as she focused on the sounds of the night. The whinny of a horse not too far behind her pricked her ears. She squeezed her thighs, pressing the mare to quicken the pace. *Solus* instantly responded and veered toward the edge of the trees, breaking into a gallop.

After another hour, dense forest gave way to open land, dropping the temperature further. They walked through drifting snow as gloaming colored the sky in a steely blue.

The crunch beneath the mare's hooves changed to a harder noise. A loud crack followed. She looked down, her gaze tracking far off to the right. They traversed across the narrowing end of a loch covered in ice.

Nervous, she urged *Solus* forward. Her cloak blew open as the horse clambered off the dangerous surface and entered into another section of forest. A flash of red to the right caught Susanna's eye, but when she glanced back, the thick branches already hid the ice behind them.

Her breathing hitched from the close brush with disaster, and she focused her attention on her surroundings as the horse picked the easiest way through the thicker foliage. She was on her own now; a fall through ice or a tumble into a ravine would turn her flight into a pointless endeavor. Peace and safety were her primary goals—not *permanent* peace. *At least . . . not yet.*

Fresh pain lanced through her chest as she thought of Robert, the look of love shining in his dark eyes haunting her. She tried to redirect her thoughts, focusing on the fierce warrior that had fought for her. With great effort, she remembered his irritation and swift decisions when she'd been a threat to him and his men . . . and herself. Images drifted to how he touched her . . . and loved her.

She sighed, deep regret of her unavoidable escape at the expense of Robert's heart besieging her. She wondered if Robert would fare well; she vehemently prayed he would.

Chapter Fourteen

⌒⌢⌒

Warmth bathed Robert's face. He woke to sunlight streaming through the open window and sighed, remembering their blissful wedding night. He slid his hand over to touch Susanna but instead found a cold empty sheet. He rolled over, reaching further with his other hand. Nothing.

He sat up and squinted, trying to see beyond the blinding brightness. The entire room was empty. Confused, he stumbled from the bed and realized Susanna's dress and slippers were gone.

His thoughts drifted back to the other night when he'd raided the kitchen and brought a feast back to their bed. Susanna's playful words from last night rang into his head: *"'Tis my turn."* The idea that she'd want to surprise him to break their fast calmed him, and he smiled at the intimate moment they'd shared when he'd tempted her with foods she'd never tasted.

Unwilling to wait a moment longer to have her in his arms, he quickly dressed and went down to the kitchen. Rowena and her staff were busy preparing the midday meal.

"Have you seen Susanna?"

"No, Commander," Rowena said. The three other women in the kitchen shook their heads.

He closed his eyes, scrubbing a hand over his brow as he forced a calming breath into his lungs. "When was the last time you saw her?"

"'Twas last night," Rowena replied.

"How long have you all been here in the kitchen?"

"I arrived before sunrise," Rowena said.

Refusing to give credence to the worst possibilities, Robert backtracked into the great hall. He didn't bother going outside, as she'd never venture out among strangers alone. With systematic precision, he opened every door and searched each room, beginning in their auxiliary wing. He worked his way back to their bedchamber, which remained empty. Only two doors remained upstairs. He knocked on Brigid's, and after no reply, opened it.

Empty.

Iain and Isobel's room was the only bedchamber remaining. He pounded on the oak door, venting the panic rising from the pit of his stomach. When no one answered, he shouldered the door open.

Empty.

He rushed back down the stairs, taking them two at a time, and strode down the hall to find Iain's study door open. Laird stood at the high wooden table, examining a map. He glanced up as Robert walked in.

"Iain, have you seen Susanna?"

"Nay, I thought she was with you in her bedchamber."

"*She's nowhere in the keep.*" His voice cracked, and he took a deep breath. "Where are Lady Isobel and Brigid?"

Iain frowned deeply. "I thought *they* were in the keep."

Robert spun around and ran through the great hall. He yanked the front door open and jogged into the courtyard, frozen snow crunching beneath his feet. Iain appeared at his side seconds later.

The courtyard had several paths that had been cut into the two-foot-deep snow, and both men sprinted down the one that led to the stables. The stable boy looked up from shoveling one of the stalls and dropped his task to greet them.

"Were any horses taken out today?" Robert asked.

"Nay," the boy replied.

Robert turned and stepped out of the structure, scanning

the courtyard. A few children played by the cottages. Uilleam, the woodcutter, led his horse and cart in over the drawbridge, carrying a load of firewood.

"But Lady Isobel and Lady Brigid took *Solus* out . . . late last night."

On Robert's left, a deep growl came from Iain, and they slowly turned back around.

"What?" Iain asked through clenched teeth.

"I tried to stop them. Brigid assured me Lady Isobel would not be riding."

"Have. They. Returned?" Iain asked.

"I doona know, Laird. I tried to wait for them, but fell asleep. *Solus* is not here."

Their heavy boots echoed over the wooden floorboards as they stormed down the stalls. Suddenly governed by their strategic minds, which fired out prioritized tasks with lightning speed, Robert tossed a saddle onto his horse and cinched the strap as Iain did the same with *Dubhar*.

"That insolent woman." Iain growled. "I shall chain her to the damn bed."

Robert put a foot into the stirrup and swung his leg over the saddle before he realized Iain had spoken of Isobel. He glanced at his friend. "You think that'll be effective?"

Iain sighed as he mounted his stallion. "Nay, but in my current mood it seems like a good plan. And . . . would make *me* happy for a while."

Robert snorted as he rode his horse into the courtyard. When Iain veered off toward the gatehouse, he followed. The guard leaned down to them from the tower window.

Iain shouted up to the guard, "Have Lady Isobel and Brigid returned?"

"Aye. They walked in on foot a short while ago." He pointed toward the great oak tree that overlooked the stream. Two figures sat beneath the tree's winter-bared branches.

Robert shouted up at the guard. "They were alone? No other woman was with them?"

"Nay. Only the two ladies. They left with Lady Isobel's warhorse but returned without it," he called down.

Robert tugged on the reins of his horse, turning toward the drawbridge. "Susanna's not safe outside our walls," he snarled, furious that his unfinished business with Dougal now exposed Susanna to harm.

"See to your woman. I'll deal with mine," Iain said.

Robert nodded and tore off across the drawbridge. He took a hard left, following the curtain wall that surrounded the castle as he followed his instincts and the lasses' clear trail. As he rounded the far corner, he came across a large area of disturbance in the snow outside their hidden underground entrance.

He urged his horse forward at a gallop, following *Solus's* tracks as they led away from Castle Brodie, racing off in the same general direction Susanna had been headed when he first encountered her. He feared a part of Susanna, even if on a subconscious level, had been half a heartbeat away from bolting in panic the entire time she'd been with him, irrespective of the grave risk to her safety.

The hard-headed woman needed to realize what was important in this world.

The things that you run toward . . .

As Susanna and *Solus* topped a gradual rise, the choking foliage of the forest thinned, allowing narrow shafts of morning light to dance down through the treetops. Sparse vegetation gave way to open rocky ground, and a low stone wall appeared beyond a thicket of bramble. Past the wall and farther up the rise, a modest stone building came into view, its frosted windowpanes perched beneath large twisted icicles that hung from a steeply pitched wood-shingled roof.

The sound of another horse whinny not far behind her quickened her pulse. She urged *Solus* forward and beyond the building to the stables around the back. She quickly found a stall for *Solus*, tied her there, and ran to the back entrance of the building. The place resembled the sanctuary her mother had described, based on long-winded stories from traveling monks.

Thankfully, the nondescript oak door on the back of the building was unlocked. Susanna slipped inside, but the door made a loud thud when she shoved it closed. It had an iron crossbar fitted across its middle, and she locked it down tight.

She strode through the kitchen into a main room where small candles flickered in alcoves and on narrow tables along the walls. A giant wooden cross to her right shadowed her as she rushed through the benches lining either side of a center aisle.

The front door, although wider than the back, had a similar crossbar. She bolted it shut as well. In seconds, the sounds of not one, but several horses could be heard beyond the door, along with the deep timbres of men's voices.

"You cannot hide from the world, my child."

She spun around to see a man kneeling at one of the tables. His back remained toward her as he lit a candle with a long stick. She stared at him while catching her breath. His robe and hair were different than Father John's. He wore a plain brown robe tied at the waist with a thin braided cord, and his hair had been trimmed short along the sides except for a circular shaved spot on top of his shiny head.

A monk. I am at the right place.

Not wanting to alert the men outside to their presence, she stepped closer to him before speaking. "But I can hide for now, can I not?"

He partially turned and sat on a bench behind him, his round face with pink cherub cheeks smiling at her. "Aye. We all have the need for refuge from the world from time to time."

A rattling sound echoed into the room, and they both looked toward the front door. Loud thumps followed, the rusted hinges squeaking and rattling in protest.

The monk turned on the bench, swinging his legs fully around. She lowered herself next to him, dropping her head to stare at his leather-booted feet beneath the brown robe.

"Will the door hold?" she whispered.

"I doona know," he whispered back. "'Twill depend on

how badly they want in."

She took a deep breath and glanced toward the door again as voices rumbled intermittently outside. Dark shapes moved before one of the paned windows, but she couldn't make out any details. She prayed that her pursuer's view inside the building was blurred to the same degree.

Another rattling and more furious pounding happened at the back door. Her pulse accelerated. Robert and his men wouldn't take her by force, would they?

The monk put his hand over hers. She'd been fisting the material of her cloak so hard, her knuckles had gone white. As she exhaled and relaxed her grip, he patted the top of her hand.

"God's will be done, child," he said.

In resignation, she gave a slow nod.

"Susanna!" A deep raspy bellow shouted out.

Her breath caught. Robert hadn't found her.

Her father had.

"If you doona come out here like a good lass, I'll be forced to come in. Doona make your great offence to me and our clan any worse."

She bit her lip and closed her eyes. Her past had hunted her down and caught her. Was escape from it not possible? She shook her head, denying the roots of hopelessness any foundation to take hold.

Silence ensued, transforming into an eerie calm that sent chills up her spine. A distorted shadow went by the window from front to back. Another dark shape followed.

Images of her and Mama cowered in the tiny bedchamber where she'd been imprisoned her entire life flashed through her mind. The waiting was the worst. When one knew an inevitable outcome was about to pass, the minutes that ticked by became tortuous hours. Susanna's leg bounced in nervous anticipation.

No more fear.

"Do you have any weapons, Father?" she glanced at him.

Kind brown eyes met her gaze as he smiled. "Nay. This is a place of safety. A house of peace not war."

She stood, restless. No longer worried about being seen,

she searched the place for anything to use in defense. Tables and benches, goblets and candles filled the front room, but the cross bearing the crucified Christ looked substantial. She glanced back through the room toward the front door. Although she and the monk might manage to drag the enormous wooden carving to bar the front door, they'd be exhausted by the effort. And by that time, the back door would be broken down.

In the kitchen, she found all they needed: jeweled daggers used for eating and a large knife. She fastened one dagger to the top of her boot with a strip of leather and held the other weapons, one in each hand.

With a steadying breath, she returned to the main hall. Her companion had already stood from his bench and paced the length of the center aisle.

"Here, Father." She tossed him the knife.

The monk caught the handle with the blade pointing down and spun it in his hand, pulling his arm to his side, bracing his legs in a wide stance. He lowered his gaze, staring through the front door.

She looked at him in amazement. "You've held a blade before?"

He gave her a sidelong glance. "I haven't always been a monk."

"Thank God for small blessings," she said.

Silence continued. No further shadows appeared near any of the windows. The sun's first rays pierced the corner of the window nearest the front.

What are they doing out there?

Too much time had gone by. If they'd planned to force the door, they would've done it by now. She inhaled deeply, scanning the windows for signs of movement, ready for anything.

A flash appeared in the window a split second before an object crashed through the glass. Another window shattered directly opposite them.

Large stones toppled some of the candles, and the flames ignited the cloth runners beneath them. Susanna stood in shock, watching as the dry wood burst into flames, setting the tables on fire. Choking black smoke rapidly filled the room. She coughed and put her sleeve up to her face as she ran back to the kitchen to look for some water. A filled bucket sat beside the door.

She wound the second dagger into the belt at her waist and lifted the bucket. Some of the water sloshed out as she struggled to carry its weight into the main room.

The monk ripped a tapestry from the wall and batted the flames with it. Nearing the tremendous heat alarmed her, but with her hands on either side of the bucket, she threw her arms forward and tossed the small amount of water onto the raging flames nearest her.

The blaze continued in spite of their efforts, mocking them. They only had a few minutes to leave through one of those doors or be engulfed in fire.

Acrid smoke burned her eyes and singed her nostrils. She pulled her cloak over her face, unable to breathe any other way.

A resounding decision formed clear in her mind as she gripped the hilt of the dagger at her waist. She would rather try everything and die fighting than admit defeat.

"Weel, Father, it would seem 'tis God's will for us to go into battle today," she said.

"Aye," he replied.

The monk dropped the tattered, smoldering tapestry and raced to the back door. She followed, tightening her hold on the hilt of her weapon, ready for anything. He lifted the crossbar, kicked open the door, and they ran out, thick black smoke furling out with them.

As the black smoke dissipated in the freezing air, there he stood—her greatest enemy.

"Broc." She spat out his name, the very sound vile on her tongue.

Long, dark-brown hair curled wildly around her father's scarred face. He stood ten feet away with his arms crossed, an evil glare leveled at her. Susanna narrowed her eyes at her lifelong demon, hatred pulsing fast through her veins.

"You ungrateful chit. Drop that ridiculous weapon," he said.

"Nay," she purred with calm venom. "I'm not goin' with you."

All of a sudden, a painful grip seized her upper arms, and she dropped the dagger. Fetid breath crawled across her cheek and filled her nostrils. "'Tis true. You'll be goin' with me."

Dougal.

Anger, fear, and a lifetime of resentment rose up from the pit of her stomach and exploded out in an animalistic sound that ripped out from her throat. Every muscle in her body snapped taut at once. She punched hard between Dougal's legs, whirled around when he bent and loosened his hold, and pulled the dagger from her boot, ramming it into the side of his neck.

He looked up at her in wide-eyed shock, a gurgling noise coming from his throat.

She ran.

The open ten-stall stable was the only other building, and she sprinted into the shelter and slammed the door shut. She spun around, her heart thundering in her ears as she stared at a door that had no lock.

Shafts of light streaming between rotting roof slats and a glow from the back wall's grimy window cast enough light to look around. She discovered a stack of freshly cut boards in the corner and dragged one over, lifted one end, and propped it against the door. Uncertain if the one would hold, she pulled another over and wedged it tightly down beside the first. She stared at the boards, hoping the creative brace held.

Robert's stallion broke through the dense forest on Brodie's neighboring lands, jumped over a broken stone wall, and descended into a swirling black smoke that billowed thickest from behind a weathered monastery. As he charged through the choking haze tainting the air, he passed five horses tied to a post in the side courtyard. He squinted when a flash of blinding sunlight glinted off an ornate bridle on the nearest animal.

Dougal.

A low shout and a clash of metal announced the location of an ongoing fight, and as Robert's stallion leaned into a turn at the back corner of the structure, he launched from his mount. In midair he unsheathed his sword, a low ring marking his presence before his boots hit the snow at a run toward the fray.

Time slowed into a series of split seconds as he analyzed the tense scene. A body lay near the back entrance of the monastery. A brown-robed monk yanked a sword from the chest of a falling man then spun, charging two others. The monk's wild-eyed glare flicked between the soldiers as he growled, his rabid spitting snarls forcing the pair to spread wide. The last behemoth warrior, who stalked toward the stables, turned back to face Robert. A deep, puckered scar marred his sinister face, running from his left temple, through his bushy eyebrow, and along a crooked nose, ending in a split at the corner of his sneering lip.

"Broc."

The MacEalan laird grunted as he unsheathed his sword, squaring off with Robert.

With instant deduction, Robert realized the body near the monastery door was Dougal's, but the cutting disappointment was brief. The satisfaction of killing Susanna's life-long tormenter would be reparation enough.

Time to even out the fight.

Robert never broke stride, sprinting through a smoke-filled area between the two buildings as he arced his weapon back and around. Broc's soldiers glanced at Robert racing by, but the monk seized on the ideal distraction and lunged, running his sword through one unlucky man.

Broc was ready for Robert's intentionally telegraphed attack and blocked with his sword. Unkempt, curly hair swirled behind the tyrant's shoulder as he turned and arced around a blow of his own.

Robert blocked the expected strike. Blade quivered against blade, sending vibrations into the bones of his arm and a deafening ring reverberating into his ears.

Broc backed away and circled around. His narrowing gaze judged Robert, assessing the worth of his unforeseen attacker.

Robert's innate observation skills, honed with a lifetime of training, translated Broc's every habitual weight shift and muscle twitch, recognizing favoritism in movements as hidden weaknesses to be exploited. "Your reign as abuser ends now."

Broc's arrogant smile stretched appallingly wide on his ugly face, a twisted laugh preceding his graveled voice. "Who are you to say?"

Robert snorted and grinned, slowly lowering his weapon as he took measured steps toward his nemesis. Noticing Broc's muscles relax infinitesimally and head tilt slightly, he teased further curiosity from him by relaxing his stance and titling his head, mirroring Broc.

One step away from deadly reach, Robert held his ground to deliver the delightful news. "I'm Susanna's husband."

Broc subtly leaned back, his jaw dropping a fraction.

Robert sprang forward, closing the distance during Broc's last heartbeat, and thrust the cold steel of delivered vengeance through his callous heart.

In a last reflex with shock-widened eyes, Broc dropped his sword and gripped the edges of Robert's blade. His lips formed a tight open circle as if a word hung there, frozen in time.

As the life faded from his rightfully tortured eyes, Robert spoke the last words Broc would ever hear. "The beginnin' of Susanna's life will now be celebrated. *Yours* is already forgotten."

Susanna remained frozen in place behind the stable door, her breath held until pain forced her to suck air into her lungs, the occasional clang of steel and muffled grunts elevating her anxiety. She guessed the monk had engaged her father in battle, but even if he'd managed to steal Dougal's sword, he still stood against four ruthless warriors. She made a silent prayer for the monk who'd shown surprising ability with a blade.

As quickly as the commotion began, it ended. After waiting but hearing nothing, she put her ear against the roughhewn surface of the door and closed her eyes in concentration.

A distant low mumble.

The crunching of snow.

Silence.

Solus nickered softly. She swallowed hard.

A pound on the door vibrated against her cheekbone and into her ear, and she jumped, startled. She glanced back at the grime-covered window and the tinder-dry walls of her hiding place, grimacing. Images of the fire she'd barely escaped threatened her without a single flame.

Determination rose up within her like no other force she'd ever known. Memories of Mama and Robert flashed into her mind. Good memories. Fragments of stolen time had brought her brief moments of happiness in a tragic life—and yet, they were enough.

She had lived and she had loved . . . and *she'd been loved.*

A lone tear drifted down her cheek as she remembered Robert staring down at her with the emotion blazing fiercely in his eyes. Her breath caught as she focused on his image, making certain Robert's face was what she held onto until the bitter end.

She took a deep fortifying breath and shouted, "Set the place afire! I doona care. I'll burn alive in here before I go anywhere with you!"

Another snow-crunched step. A single soft thud on the door.

"Susanna. Let me in."

She gasped.

Robert!

"I promise not to take you anywhere, but please let me in. If you're going to burn alive in there . . . let my body be the one to shield you and set you ablaze."

Her throat seized at his words. Tears streamed freely down her cheeks as she struggled to move the first board aside. It fell to the earthen ground with a hollow thud. She kicked the other one aside, impatient to free the door.

She grasped the iron handle and yanked the door open. Robert's forehead rested on the door, and he stumbled into her open arms.

"My father? Dougal?" She leaned to the side, glancing around, trying to see beyond him.

He moved, blocking her view. "Nay, Susanna. They'll not bother you again. I killed Broc. Dougal had already been felled by a dagger plunged into his throat."

She raised her hand, covering her mouth. "What of the monk?"

"Doona worry about any of them. The monk killed the others and is removin' the mess your father and his men created.

As he scanned her features, concern etched into his face, his brows furrowing. "Susanna, you're blackened. Are you harmed?" He stepped back, pulling her arms wide.

"Nay, Robert. I'm hale and whole."

A hand touched her face with the gentleness of a feather. His dark eyes bored down into hers. The handsome face she'd imagined, the last memory she wanted to hold onto when she left this world, now stood before her . . . *had saved her.*

His face softened. "Aye, that you are. Us . . . *together* . . . makes me whole too."

Chapter Fifteen

The moment Susanna had smiled up at him, Robert's upside-down world had been set right again. With glistening tear tracks across the cheeks of a soot-covered face, her hair a tangled mess, and a gown ripped and torn, she looked up at him as if he'd just delivered an entire world of hope to her . . . and he'd never seen a more beautiful sight.

"Lass, I nearly died when I found you'd gone."

Her head tilted downward, fresh tears streaming down her dirty cheeks. "Robert, I'm so sorry. I dinna feel I had any other choice. It pains me greatly to know I hurt you."

He tucked a finger under her chin, lifting her face. "Nay, Susanna. 'Tis I who failed you. We've much to discuss. When we're through, you'll have a choice of where you go. You shall always have the choice. Know this, though. I'll never take a solid breath in this world unless I know you are safe. I hope you'll want that safety with me, under all the love and protection I'm able to provide."

"What if I canna stay there, Robert? I tried. Everythin' closed in . . . 'til I could no longer breathe."

"My place is with you now, Susanna. I go where you go. We can live under the blanket of the stars if you like, the sun our only daytime family. But if we talk about everythin'—if you give me the chance to explain the unbelievable things you witnessed back at the castle—I think you'll decide to go back and try again."

She sighed. A small smile tugged at the corners of her mouth. "I *do* like Isobel and Brigid."

"Better friends you'll never find," he said, pulling her gently into his embrace.

"You have a cottage. But what if I'd rather live in the bedchamber they'd given me?"

He snorted. "Lass, I would clear out every room in Iain's castle for you if doin' so would make you happy, and I'd gladly suffer the severe repercussions of such a feat. I only hope you'd want me there with you to warm your bed."

She laughed, and the sound calmed him to a degree. Overwhelming panic at losing her had nearly stopped his heart, but now that he held his entire world in his arms, anything was possible.

"Come, lass." He turned her back into the stable toward Lady Isobel's mare, needing to lead her far away from the place that she'd run to and begin her on the journey where she belonged. By his side.

Susanna paused after they took a few steps, and he wondered at her hesitation. His heart had nearly burst from his chest at the sight of her alive and safe; but being with her alone washed a peace and happiness through him like nothing he'd ever imagined.

Overcome by raw emotion, he lifted the red ribbon from behind the folds in his tartan. "I found this—" his voice broke "—it was lyin' on the ice." He held it out to her.

Her gaze drifted to the ribbon, and Susanna pulled the silken fabric into her hand. She stared down at it, motionless.

Robert waited as the silence stretched out, but he began to grow concerned that he'd upset her.

"I choose you, Robert," she whispered.

The soft-spoken words resonated into his ears like a God-given gift.

"You do?"

"Aye." She turned around, gazing up at him. "Help me deal with the demons in my mind . . . and I promise never to run from you again."

He blew out a held breath and smiled down at her. "And

I vow: if you panic and break your promise, I'll chase after you."

"And convince me to return with you?" She raised her delicate eyebrows, those mesmerizing blue eyes sparkling beneath them.

"Nay, my love. I'll be wherever you are. I'll protect you. I'll offer all that I am to you. Wherever you are—"

Susanna raised a finger and placed it over his lips, silencing him. Her smile grew wider.

"Wherever you are ... I am found. You're the one I wished for. I prayed for you long before I met you." She cupped her hand over his cheek, fresh tears brimming in her eyes.

"Susanna, I wished for *us* under that mistletoe."

She leaned up against him, entwining her hands around his neck as he dipped his head down. She placed the softest kiss on his lips. As he closed his eyes, losing himself in their tender connection, drifting as close to Heaven as God allowed a man to get, her lips curved into a smile.

Sweet words drifted from her lips, branding his heart.

"Then *us* we shall forever be."

Epilogue

Six days later . . .

Susanna nestled further back into her seat. Robert growled into her ear as he hardened further beneath her. He tightened his arms around her, rendering her immobile. "Hold still, lass."

She smiled and wiggled her hips in defiance.

His lips brushed over the shell of her ear and paused with a gentle kiss. The low timbre of his threat followed. "Doona tempt me. I've half a mind to drag you upstairs the next time you move."

"Only half a mind?" she teased.

His arms tightened, and she froze.

"Fine. I concede." She turned her head back, glancing at him. "For now."

His deep chuckle rumbled through her back. "I do enjoy your spirit, woman."

A sudden squeal of joy erupted across from them. Susanna settled back into Robert's arms and watched as Isobel pulled the wrapping from her present.

The Christmas tree sparkled, the tiny candles in glass jars dangling from its branches causing all the silver ornaments to flicker with light. Susanna's gaze fell beneath the tree, which had somehow exploded with presents overnight; linen and silk wrapped shapes with red and gold bows reached up into the branches and overflowed onto the wooden floor.

The mysterious dark angel stood in the far corner of the room, a smug look on his face, his arms crossed over his broad bare chest. Susanna wasn't sure if her eyes played tricks on her—after the amazing revelations Robert had shared over the last few days, she'd likely always trust her eyesight—but she swore a slight smile twitched at the corners of his mouth. Intuition told her the angel was responsible for the appearance of the presents, at least in part.

Isobel turned fully toward the angel. "My Kindle? With . . . a solar charger?"

The tops of his massive wings rose with his impassive shrug. "How else would you read it here?"

Iain snatched it from her hand.

Isobel growled. "That's my present. Get your own."

"You keep this only on the condition that the *electronic item in the thirteenth century* is merely borrowed. And read in private. And kept under lock and key."

Isobel gave her husband a deadpan expression. "Really. That's what you want to lock up? Leave your study door wide open, inviting the whole world in to snoop around the magick of this place, but you want to lock up my coveted romance library?"

Iain tugged her down onto his lap, and Isobel fell back awkwardly. "I'll give you all the romance you will ever need, woman."

"But I can keep it?" she asked him.

"On well-guarded loan," he reiterated. "The magick of the castle may not be historically known, but I won't allow a technological advancement to remain here, in an improper time period, for long."

Isobel grinned broadly as Susanna witnessed the puzzling exchange along with everyone else. The meaning of what they talked about escaped her, but she was growing accustomed to learning things in bits and pieces with all of the wonders within Brodie Castle.

"Thank you, Skorpius," Isobel chimed out in sing-song.

Another shrug lifted the angel's black wings. His eyes had locked onto Brigid, who seemed to be doing her best to ignore his presence.

Isobel smirked. "It's official. I'm done with Cupid. I'm now calling you Santa Claus."

Skorpius's iridescent blue-green eyes rolled toward the ceiling and stayed there as he sighed. "Delightful. Of course you are."

Iain laughed at the angel's last remark, the deep sound filling the room. Everyone joined in, the joy in the room contagious.

Only members of Iain's immediate family were here during the early hours of the Christmas morning. Isobel and Iain were nearest the tree. Gawain, acting thoroughly bored, yet watching everyone, sat on the other side of Brigid. Susanna and Robert were present by default due to their living within the keep, but she suspected by her husband's closeness with Laird Iain, that they were more like family than friends.

To Susanna's surprise, two small children wearing linen gowns crept up barefooted beside Brigid's chair. Both of them had long, blond curls. One looked to be a boy perhaps, but she couldn't tell for certain. Susanna glanced at Robert, wondering why in all the days she'd been here, she hadn't noticed any wee ones wandering about the keep, yet here two were. They looked no older than four summers, one standing a bit taller than the other.

A fleeting memory teased her mind. Brigid in the dark corridor on Susanna's wedding night, upset about Skorpius vanishing, and someone else . . . and *the children*.

"Lady Brigid?" The little girl spoke, her tiny hand resting on Brigid's forearm.

Brigid turned, shock registering over her face. "Connell! Gunna!" She sprung out of her chair and wrapped her arms around the children, lifting them into the air as all three squealed.

"Mmm-hmmm . . ." Isobel said. "Santa Claus."

Susanna glanced back toward the angel, but he'd disappeared. She tightened her grip around Robert's arms, and he gave her a tight squeeze while resting his lips against the shell of her ear.

She hummed as warmth spread from a deep ache in her chest. "Robert, you've told me of Isobel's travels through time and of the magick of your castle, with powerful, castle-hidin' walls and the angels beyond them. But you dinna tell me the greatest magick was right here." She nodded toward the family.

"Aye, lass. 'Tis not the greatest, though."

"Nay?" she asked.

The loud excitement of the room drifted away as she focused on the warrior who held her. She shifted within his arms, turning sideways on his lap. His dark hair fell in a silken curtain around his face. A faded scar beside his left eyebrow beckoned her, and she kissed it softly. "What is the greatest magick?"

"'Tis a miracle, rather. That two people who'd given up hope of findin' love in this world, collided together." His warm breath whispered across her cheek.

She kissed him with reverent tenderness and closed her eyes. "Aye. 'Tis a miracle. 'Tis a wish granted. 'Tis a prayer answered."

Robert dropped his forehead, resting it on hers. "Know one thing. If you never know another thing in this world to be true, know this now and forever, Susanna."

He lifted his hands, sliding his fingers into her hair and cradling the back of her head. He held her with his strong arms wrapping around her, his kind heart emanating from his gentle actions, his voice dropping low, uttering the most powerful words.

"You are loved."

ABOUT THE AUTHOR

Kat Bastion is an award-winning paranormal romance writer, poetic warrior, and eternal optimist who loves getting lost in the beauty of nature.

On a never-ending, wondrous path of self-discovery, Kat throws her characters into incredible situations with the hope that readers join her in learning more about the meaning of life and love.

Her first published work, *Utterly Loved*, was shared with the world to benefit others. All proceeds from *Utterly Loved*, and a portion of the proceeds from all her other books, support charities who help those lost in this world.

Kat lives with her husband amid the beautiful Sonoran Desert of Arizona.

Visit her blog at www.talktotheshoe.com, her website at www.katbastion.com, and her Twitter account at https://twitter.com/KatBastion for more information.

LOOK FOR THE NEXT HIGHLAND LEGENDS
NOVEL

Born of

MIST *and* LEGEND

WINTER, 2014

Printed in Great Britain
by Amazon